Alexis,
I hope you enjoy
Varrick's story,

Varrick's Disturbances

A Novel by
Patrick Rowlee

This book is dedicated to
both of my fathers...

Robert Emerson Rowlee (1926-1962)

And

Yahweh

ACKNOWLEDGMENTS

I would like to acknowledge the support and assistance of several people, beginning with Sandy Thornton who spent many hours on the design, layout, and final assembling of Varrick's Disturbances in preparation for this printing; my good friends Sue Peck and Paul Lankovsky for their considerable patience, consultative skills, and good humor when I started entertaining ambitions of actually writing down thoughts and stories for publication; Mary Somers, close friend of my wife and mine for close to thirty years (yikes!) for her feedback, wisdom, and "left field" sense of humor; my mother and father for their enormous impact on my life; my students who have encouraged me with their youthful enthusiasm and interest in this project; and, finally, the wonderful woman with whom I have spent the last twenty-seven years of wedded bliss for her input, support, encouragement, photographic assistance, and – most of all – love, my wife and biggest supporter Linda. A special thank you, of course, to my muse, Buckshot Northern Skye!

--- Patrick Rowlee

Chapter

1

It was 1965 and my Little League team was practicing. Our Eagles were playing on one of the baseball diamonds at Yuccaville High School, preparing for our season opener. Since it was March in the Mojave Desert, it was 'as cold as a witch's heart,' according to our manager Mr. Rodriguez. He pronounced witch's as weechez. Because Coach had a Mexican accent, he had a habit of pronouncing a soft-I as a long-E sound.

We were practicing on a field bordered by the chain-link fence that marked the north border of the campus. The wind blew like crazy, practically knocking me down at my post in center field. Every shred of my will was needed to keep my four-foot-ten, eighty-pound frame from falling backwards. Standing in the teeth of the forty-mile-an-hour wind wearing a thin windbreaker for warmth was enough challenge for an eleven-year-old, but the fact we weren't close to finishing and there hadn't been a ball hit my way yet was too much to bear.

So, I did what I have always done whenever things get boring - I began imagining: There I was, standing in center field at Yankee Stadium and wearing the uniform of my beloved Yanks, the number seven emblazoned on the back of my pinstriped jersey, the numeral of the greatest player to don any baseball uniform - the great Mickey Mantle. Whitey Ford stood on the mound, wound, and threw a 3-2 fastball at my second-favorite ballplayer, the 'Say Hey Kid' - the wonderfully magnificent Willie Mays.

Willie swung at Whitey's knee-high fastball and applied a ton of wood to it, propelling the ball high and toward my general direction.

I drew a bead on it and took off as quickly as my osteomylitis-diseased hip would allow. The crowd in 'The House That Ruth Built' roared as I turned for the wall and tracked the ball over my left shoulder. Back, back, back I raced, determined to flag down Willie's prodigious fly and save the day for the Yanks in the seventh game of the World Series. However, as I sprinted toward the wall awaiting 'Mr. Spalding' to whiz my way, I heard my name. Figuring it was the crowd chanting 'Mickey, Mickey,' I tried blotting it out. After all, I couldn't stop to acknowledge my fans in the middle of the very play that could decide the Series.

As I leapt to keep Willie's blast from sailing over the fence and the streaking ball was about to land in my outstretched glove, the yelling of my name became too much. I had no choice but to acknowledge it, even though I would likely miss the ball and therefore lose the Series for my beloved Bronx Bombers.

"What?" I yelled in exasperation. "What do you want?"

I stopped short and faced home plate, allowing the Giants to win and swarm onto the field.

"Eets time for you to bat, O'Connell," my manager yelled. "Unless you think you don't need it."

I blinked twice before recognizing reality. I looked down at my nylon windbreaker and blue jeans. I smiled shyly and ran toward home plate.

Mr. Rodriguez shook his head and yelled, "You're always dreaming, amigo. Can't spend your whole life in the clouds, you know."

Even though my cheeks burned from the dry, frigid wind, I felt a second sensation - the warming of my forehead that occurred whenever I became embarrassed, which was quite often back in 1965.

I grabbed the closest bat so as not to waste any more time, a 28-ounce Louisville Slugger too small even for me, but I didn't want to agitate Coach Rodriguez. I ran to the batter's box, took one quick swing, and dug in.

The batting practice pitcher was Coach's son Louie, who was much larger and older than any of us Eagles. He helped with practice since none of the players' fathers ever volunteered. The other teams had plenty of coaches, but none of the Eagle fathers would help Mr. R. He was liked by all of us boys, but wasn't respected by the adults. Why, I didn't know at the time, but I had overheard them making disparaging remarks. They called him 'Beaner' and 'Spick' and laughed whenever he spoke to the team.

Louie Rodriguez usually did something on the mound to make me laugh, so it was hard to concentrate as I prepared for the first pitch. "Stee-rike one!" Mr. Rodriguez bellowed before I could react.

A voice from left field yelled, "Come on, Varrick. You can do it." It was Jack Bryant, my best friend. Jack had a knack for knowing how and when to prod me to do better.

I waggled the bat twice, squinted so hard that all I could see was Louie, and waited for the next pitch. He wound in the high-kick delivery he copied from Camilo Pascual of the Chicago White Sox and hurled a fastball thigh-high and just outside. My right foot stepped toward the mound and my hips exploded as I swung the 28-ouncer with all the fury my bony body could muster. I stretched for the ball in order to compensate for the outside location and the short club.

The ball connected with the fattest part of the bat, where it begins to round at the end. Because of my point of contact and the freezing cold conditions, my hands were zapped a serious shock. But that didn't matter to me because I had just made great contact against a kid three years older.

Since I bat left and got around a little late on Louie's heater, the ball shot toward the left-field foul line. My buddy Jack took off immediately for it. He didn't race after it nearly as fast as I had in my reverie of a few moments before, but he made better time than most ten-year-olds. He had long, skinny legs built for speed. That's what I told him whenever I tried cheering him up. And he usually needed cheering up. I wouldn't know exactly why until later that season.

Jack streaked toward the ball, but it flew at least eight feet above his outstretched glove. He then stopped in his tracks and pulled something only he could get away with - he threw his mitt at the ball. Everyone on our team busted up laughing, even Mr. Rodriguez. Jack just looked toward home with a helpless look on his freckled face and shrugged like Jack Benny. His body language seemed to say, 'What am I supposed to do? The guy blasted it. No one could've caught up with it, not Roger Maris, not Mickey Mantle, not even Willie Mays.'

Jack Bryant was not the kind of kid a manager could get mad at, and

11

this was even before we all found out about Jack's condition that cut his life short.

I don't remember much else of that long-ago practice, but I will never forget Jack running like the wind and throwing his Frank Howard fielder's glove as if it had a chance of catching the ball. Whenever I think of 1965 I think of that moment. And the funny thing is, half of me laughs and half of me chokes up. It's a memory I cherish and keep with me always. Whenever I need to feel better, I play back the images of that freezing, wind-blown practice and am transported for a fleeting moment and it helps me in a way I can't explain exactly. All I know is it lifts my spirits and helps put everything back into perspective.

Chapter

2

After my batting practice homer, I figured things would start looking up. I'd been in a really long slump - not just in baseball, but in all aspects of my life. Dad had died three baseball seasons earlier and my life had been heading south ever since.

In 1965, though, I was still forgetting on occasion that my father was gone. At least one Saturday morning every month I'd wake up with the most satisfying sensation. I'd start planning how we'd spend the day together. I would muse that Dad might take me out for breakfast and then to the hobby store to look at slot cars. Or, maybe he'd surprise me and take me to an Angels' game. If the Yankees were in town, I'd get to see The Mick play. Right after I'd jump out of bed I'd stop in my tracks with the cruel memory that my father was gone forever. I'd feel both cheated and betrayed, fall onto my bed, and stare at the ceiling until Mom called me for breakfast.

The other slump I was in was baseball-related. Although I was a pretty good glove man and had one of the best throwing arms in the league, my batting left a lot to be desired. Ever since Dad died, my skills had declined significantly. Everyone in the league now seemed to know I was a soft touch. There was hardly a pitcher who didn't know of my fear of being hit. And no one knew it better than my nemesis - Ross Ramsey of the Leviathans - the most frightening hurler in Yuccaville.

The season opened with my Eagles facing Ramsey. Coach Rodriguez started me in center field even though he knew I was terrified of 'Big R.' I suspected he'd had his son Louie pitch batting practice the week before to prepare us - especially me - for our game against Ramsey.

Ever since I'd hit that screamer in practice, I had become the embodiment of optimism. As I took the field on Opening Day, I trotted out to center field with excessive confidence.

Although we were already one run behind as we ran to the dugout for our first at-bat (thanks to Big R knocking the first pitch out of the park), I brimmed with hope. After all, the weather was glorious, the birds were singing, and we were tied with the Leviathans for first. Anything could happen, I told myself. We had as much chance of winning the pennant this year as anyone.

Since I batted sixth, it was unlikely I'd have my ups in the first inning, so I began studying 'Big R.' I figured there might be a detail in his delivery that would give away which pitch he'd throw next. I sat perched on the concrete slab above our bench and chomped away on a wad of Hubba-Bubba Bubble Gum. Jack Bryant plopped down beside me and did the same. He also needed to find the key to unlock the mystery that was Ross Ramsey. Jack, too, had gone hitless the season before against him. It was a small source of pride for me that Jack had done even worse. He'd gone 0 for 10 while I had been only 0 for 9. Of course, I never pointed this out to Jack, but it gave me a measure of comfort.

"Look at that sum buck pitch," Jack gasped as Big R let loose of his first warm-up pitch. The ball hurtled toward home and made a sharp 'splat' in the catcher's mitt. A cloud of dirt burst from the leather and there was an audible gasp from the crowd, especially those seated on our side.

I swallowed hard and chewed my Hubba-Bubba faster. Big R was a head taller than any other player in the Majors and we'd heard reports his parents had had to order an extra-long bed for him. As I squinted to get a close-up of his face, I swallowed again. "I don't believe it."

"What?" Jack whispered.

"Look real close at his face."

"I'm looking. Oh my gosh, he has a beard! How old is he, anyway, twenty-five?"

"He's gotta be at least fourteen, fifteen years old."

Above his brooding lips and along his lantern jaw were clumps of dark. Not peach fuzz or an occasional hair, but patches of dark stubble. We both swallowed audibly.

14

While the uniforms of all the Eagles hung off our little shoulders, Big R's gray flannels hugged his. We wore size-small uniforms while this behemoth stretched out a double extra-large. And his feet! He wore at least a man's size fourteen. Jack and I ogled this boy-giant as if we were watching a scary movie. By the time he finished tossing his warm-ups and the ump yelled 'Play ball,' we'd lowered ourselves to the bench and slunk down low as he prepared to pitch to our leadoff batter Bunny Youngman.

Big R leaned forward to read the catcher's signal, nodded solemnly, and wound up. His right foot shot straight up in the air, way above his head. He reminded me more of Juan Marichal than a Little League twirler. His muscular left arm jerked and snapped like a bullwhip, hurtling the spheroid downward toward home. It whizzed just above Bunny's kneecaps and over the plate. "Stee-rike!" the ump bawled.

Instead of a cheer rising from the visitors' side, a blanket of silence fell over the whole park. However, moments later, Mr. Rodriguez had the foolish notion to yell through cupped hands, "That's okay, Bunny. You can heet this guy. No hay problema, Amigo."

Big R glowered at Mr. R like he'd just as soon knock him down as look at him. He smirked, tugged his cap further down over his eyes, shook off a signal, and wound more furiously than before. The second pitch was a fastball at least ten miles per hour faster that whooshed past Bunny before he could even begin to swing. From then on, our dugout was as quiet as a morgue. Seven straight blazing strikes later, Coach summoned us out of our communal stupor. "Let's hold 'em, boys." We shuffled out to our positions like subjects at a hypnotist stage show.

Since I always batted right after Jack, we were both due up in the second. We must have looked like condemned men on Death Row or something because Rodriguez yelled, "Hey, look alive, compadres. This ain't practice."

Because of my fearful, foggy state, I have absolutely no idea how we kept the Leviathans from scoring a second run. All I know is my skin crawled at the thought of facing Ross Ramsey. I hadn't felt such dread since Dad died.

Standing on-deck with one out, I turned my back on home plate for the first time in my life. I just couldn't bear to watch Jack face

Big R. All I remember was the snap of the catcher's mitt on the first two pitches. Then, I don't know what possessed me, but I spun around and yelled, "Come on, Jackie. You can definitely hit this guy."

Jack Bryant stepped out of the box and stared at me in disbelief. His face seemed to say, 'Now we're both in big trouble. This guy'll have you for breakfast unless you drop to your knees and beg for mercy."

Have you ever had a tangible sensation someone was staring at you? I felt a blast of heat like a furnace hitting my face and arms. Continuing to possess some newfound lunacy, I faced the source of the heat and looked him straight in the eye. He didn't succeed in staring me down, but I could sense my eyes beginning to fill with water.

"Play ball!" the ump bellowed.

"Yeah, play ball," I half yelled.

Jack shook his head and shot me another look as if to say, "I tried stopping you, but you won't listen. If you're going to play the fool, it's your funeral."

This only seemed to tick off Big R even more because the next pitch exceeded the others so much in velocity that the ump didn't bother bellowing "strike three."

When Jack and I met halfway, his mood switched to pity. "Good luck, Varrick. I'm praying for you," he said as he handed me the bat.

My legs were starting to quiver and my wad of Hubba-Bubba was stuck to the roof of my mouth. I sucked in the dusty air and took two warm-up swings. My pulse raced and my head felt fuzzy.

Since Ramsey and I are both lefties, I had an extra disadvantage: I got to face his hideous roundhouse curve along with his searing heat.

I finished my swings and stepped gingerly into the box. Big R then did something I'd never seen him do: he turned his back and bent over the ball. Then, after a count of ten, he spun around and stepped onto the rubber. Glaring down, he seemed to look right through me. He angrily shook off two signs and then lit up at the sight of the third. He resembled the Big Bad Wolf about to huff and puff and blow my little body down. He whirled and shot a tiny white pill out of his cannon of an arm. To my complete horror it headed straight for my head! I barely had the presence of mind to duck, and I heard it whiz right over my neck. As I stared at the ground, my first thought was that I was going to be sick.

A glob of vomit appeared at the back of my throat and burned like Mrs. Rodriguez's homemade salsa.

"Ball one," the ump intoned. It was the first time that he'd said that with Ramsey on the mound.

I stepped out of the box and took in another dusty breath. My gum was still stuck to the back of my throat. Someone somewhere was yelling encouragement, but I was so disoriented I couldn't make the words out. They were remote, yet supportive, and I sensed they were Jack's.

In contrast to the first pitch, Big R looked relaxed. By imperiling my life, he appeared to have gained a sense of peace. He looked downright placid as he looked in for the signal, and actually accepted his catcher's first suggestion. He wound slower than before and delivered from the side. The ball appeared headed three feet behind me, but made a crazy detour about ten feet away and somehow snaked by my chest. It unaccountably made it over the inside corner and "Stee-rike one" rang out.

A smirk spread across Big R's face, as he no doubt saw panic splattered over mine. His face, now bursting with confidence, troubled me more than his dominant pitching. The higher his ego soared, the lower mine plummeted. I now simply wanted to survive the ordeal without fainting. I was willing to lose dignity as my teammates had, but I didn't care to lose consciousness. So, as I gripped my thirty-ounce Mickey Mantle bat and prepared for the third pitch, I begged each breath to fill my lungs. The rest of the at-bat was a blur. All I remember is consolation spreading through my body as I jogged to center field for the top of the third.

Two more up and two more down, and the game was basically over. We lost by "only" six runs. Our small comfort was we didn't lose to the Leviathans by double digits like all the other teams in the first round would. It was a tiny consolation, but a moral victory just the same.

Chapter

3

After the game was over and we had consoled each other and cried into our snow cones, we Eagles went our separate ways. I crossed 20th Avenue and entered my neighborhood alone. Since I lived on the other end of the tract called Mountain View (which had no view of anything), I had to wend my way around several streets before I'd arrive home. As I walked down Ninth Place, I saw something more frightening than a Ross Ramsey fastball.

The Krupt Brothers - Bobby, Danny, and Tony – headed directly toward me. Terror struck, causing my entire spine to tingle. And right then, as if they smelled my fear, all three brothers noticed me. Bobby, the biggest and oldest, nudged Danny, who gave out a guffaw and poked his little brother Tony as if to say, 'Here comes that little chump O'Connell. You'd better kick his butt.'

It's amazing how many images used to rush through my brain in a few seconds whenever I was scared, how complex my imaginings would become whenever confronted, and how much my response to fear egged on my predators.

Since there was no sidewalk to retreat to, I had no choice but to walk directly toward the three approaching Blackfoot Indians. After they clumped together, I tried walking around them. However, I was quickly foiled when all three stepped laterally to the middle of the street.

"Uh uh. Where you think you're going?" Bobby asked.

"Home?" I asked in answer.

"Home?" Bobby said to Danny in a falsetto. "Home?"

Danny equaled his brother's wit by repeating my answer. "Home?"

he said. "Hear that, Tony? He wants to go 'home?'"

Tony, two inches shorter than me, but much more experienced in fighting and playing the tough guy, delivered the line with much more anger than his brothers. "Home? Home? Why home?"

Since it was the code of all kids to never answer a younger kid's demand, I ignored him. In fact, I pretended to ignore all three of them. I tried walking around Tony. As I did, he lunged at me with his left hand, but missed. He lurched forward, but just caught himself from falling down.

He must've looked funny to his brothers because they burst into laughter. Apparently finding Tony more amusing than the prospect of starting a fight with me, they lapsed into hyena-like derision of him. I dared not look back for fear that even in the midst of gut-splitting hilarity they might remember me and take chase.

Although terrified, I fought the urge to run. Ignoring my instincts, I continued walking briskly. It wasn't 'til I had almost rounded the corner that I sneaked a glance back. Bobby and Danny held their mouths and writhed in glee a full minute after their brother's faux pas.

Two minutes later, I breathlessly rounded the corner of Marina Street and headed home. We had moved to the sleepy, elm-lined street in the summer of '61, a year before my father died. Although he had been the "bread winner," my mom was able to manage paying the mortgage between her earnings as a secretary and a small settlement she received from the insurance company of the man who killed Dad.

Some drunk who'd never been in Yuccaville zigzagged down Yucca Boulevard one quiet Sunday morning and plowed directly into my father.

Dad had been standing on the median waiting for the man to pass when the driver lost control of his Lincoln. Dad flew fifty feet before striking the asphalt. He died upon impact with the boulevard's asphalt surface.

So, for two years and eight months since, my mother, sisters Deirdre and Trina, and I had somehow survived. Although, I never thought any of us survived it well.

I climbed the four steps to our front door, entered quietly, and headed directly for my room. After changing out of my uniform and into pajamas, I pulled out the couch and lay on my bed. Exhausted from the game and the run-in with the Krupts, I fell asleep. Much later, my older sister Deirdre burst in, switched on the TV, cranked the volume, and plopped down on my feet. I hollered for her to get off me, but she ignored me until I hit her with a pillow. As I writhed in pain and massaged my ankle, she went to my desk and picked up my favorite car model. "What's this? One of Varry's little models? He's not man enough to drive a real car, so he has to play with itty-bitty baby cars."

I knew what was next, but I protested anyway. "Put it back! That's my favorite model. Leave it alone."

She gave a short shriek of laughter and skipped out of the room with my Model T Roadster in hand.

"Hey, put my model back."

Re-entering seconds later with the black roadster, she peeled back the red flame decal on the passenger door, and waited for my reaction. Part of me tried ignoring her and the rest wanted to wring her neck. You can guess which part won. I struggled out of bed, but my ankle wouldn't carry me. I fell head first, just out of reach of Deirdre.

"I wonder what this'd look like without headlights."

"You better not. Give it back."

I lunged for her, but she stepped back just far enough to elude me. "What are you going to do, Sissy Boy? Tell Mummy? Oooooh, I'm frightened."

She snapped off both headlights and threw them onto my bed and then tore the rear bumper off with a flourish.

"That does it," I yelled as I lunged again. She dodged me by running out to the hallway. Placing my car on the floor, she said, "Let's see how sturdy this little fella is," and then stomped it with relish. The roof caved in and the rear wheels popped off.

I yelled at the top of my lungs, "Why did you do that, you stupid jerk?"

Suddenly, Mom appeared. "What on earth is going on?"

I was so angry I could barely form words. "Deir-deir-deirdre is ..."

"I don't care what Deirdre's doing. No one, and I mean no one, deserves to be called what I heard you all the way out in the backyard calling her. Now apologize to her right this instant. Dee, come here."

Deirdre reappeared. The roadster was nowhere in sight. She must have stowed it away for future torture sessions. Her eyes were somehow wet. "Mom, I - I - I just don't know why Varrick is so mean to me all the time."

The look on Mom's face devastated me. She was so disappointed that even *I* believed for a moment that I'd been the aggressor. I knew there was no way out. Deirdre had once again set me up. And what did I have to show for my efforts? I now had a sprained ankle and one less model in my shrinking collection.

It took all my self-control to keep from crying. What a day I had had. Between Ross Ramsey's annihilation of my team, the Krupts terrorizing me, and Big Sister rendering me lame, my world had fallen apart.

Summoning all my strength, I looked Deirdre in the eye and said, "I'm sorry I called you that name."

My mom looked back at Deirdre, who was wiping away her crocodile tears, and said to her, "Now, Dee, I want you to apologize to your brother since he apologized to you."

"Sorry," she said flatly. As soon as Mom turned to look at me, Deirdre stuck out her tongue and bugged her eyes. I realized I was a beaten man, so I didn't bother protesting.

All I really wanted was to be left alone, so I ignored Dee and asked Mom to close my door. As soon as she did, I lay on my bed and opened a Casper the Friendly Ghost comic book. For some reason, stories about ghosts and angels relaxed me. I've always had an interest in both, but angels are somehow more fascinating. Ever since I can remember, I've believed that everyone has his own guardian angel. Little did I know my belief would cause me so much grief.

Chapter

4

Although I was a good student, I didn't like school all that much. The teachers were nice and most of the students liked me, but there was a group I was *very* unpopular with - the bullies. Since I was the best boy student in my grade, I was a marked man or sitting duck for every Tom, Dick, or Harry who resented my achievement in the classroom.

Bobby Krupt was the worst. He was the most feared student at Joshua School. All Bobby had to do was show up and kids would instantly shut up. Giggling girls stifled themselves and guys who were regular smart Alecks were suddenly stricken speechless and only spoke if Bobby spoke to them. Bobby hadn't beaten up a single person...yet; but he had the reputation of being the meanest, most dangerous kid to walk our campus. Even high school kids avoided him.

Bobby had slugged a kid at his last school for refusing to give him a pencil. A man teacher supposedly came over to try to pull Bobby off the boy. Bobby punched the teacher once in the nose and once in the jaw, breaking both. The school board expelled him. His family moved to Yuccaville so Bobby could attend school. I guess it's a law that if you're from out of state you can't be denied an education, even if you've been expelled.

On his first day of school, when our sixth-grade teacher Mrs. Regal introduced him, Bobby received a good reception. The girls swooned when he stood and fixed his gaze on them. His coal-black hair and piercing eyes reminded them of Tonto from the popular TV show 'The Lone Ranger.' Since he stood taller than our teacher and weighed one-thirty, we figured he was a good athlete. Playing the role of ambassador since I was class president, I introduced myself and welcomed him.

Mrs. Regal then announced we were having a spelling bee. Half the class lined up on each side of the room and she began reading off words from our spelling list.

When she got to Bobby, Mrs. Regal conceded, "Since Bobby is new and we want to welcome him properly, I will give him a word from the first chapter."

Flipping to the front of the speller, she squinted for a moment and then brightened. "Spelling," she uttered.

I was embarrassed for our newest classmate; embarrassed he'd been asked to spell such an easy word. So, I blew hard on my lips and made a Bronx cheer. A few of the kids laughed. Bobby turned quickly and glared at me, then at them. That's when we all knew we were in trouble.

Bobby narrowed his eyes and looked down and said, "Spelling." He took several seconds to think it over and then said, "S-P-E-L," before pausing a moment and finishing with "I-N-G." A gasp rose from the class as we heard him misspell the easiest word in our book. What made it even easier was that it was emblazoned across the front cover of the orange paperback Mrs. Regal held at chest level and the words 'Spelling Bee' had been printed in five-inch letters on the chalkboard. A kid with his street smarts should've figured the easy way out, but he was either too nervous or clueless to cheat. And if he had, Mrs. Regal would've either been fooled or never let on. Instead, it was apparent to everyone that Bobby Krupt, the largest kid in the sixth grade, was its worst speller. Not even Kathy Wilhoit, the girl with the perpetual smile who left everyday for two hours of 'special education,' would've missed 'spelling.'

Mrs. Regal pursed her lips. "I'm sorry, Bobby, that's incorrect." She said softly, "Have a seat, please."

His face turned crimson. He lowered his head and shuffled to his seat with both hands jammed into his pants pockets. I hoped someone would misspell a word just to break the tension, but no one did. Mrs. Regal looked like she hoped someone would join Bobby in the middle of the room.

Later that day, when I held the door for Bobby as our class headed out for recess, he brushed past and stuck an elbow in my solar plexus, knocking all of the wind out of me. I must've turned white because a kid passing by asked, "What's wrong, Varrick? You look like you just saw a ghost."

From that day on, there was no peace. Wherever I went, I kept a lookout for him. I retreated more and more into myself at school and even around home. My stomach was always in knots. I rarely visited the restroom at school for fear any or all three Krupts would jump me.

The next few months were a nightmare. My sister Deirdre heard me talking in my sleep and calling out the Krupts' names. She teased me mercilessly, such as handing me the phone and saying, "It's for you. Someone named Bobby." Or, if I said I was going somewhere, she'd chide, "I hear Bobby'll be there. Do you really want to get beat up?"

The taunts continued until a cold January day when Mrs. Regal welcomed another new student to our class, Larry Jasper. Larry stood five feet, nine inches and weighed at least 150. He was the most muscular kid I'd ever seen. You'd think since he was larger than Bobby everyone in class would receive him with open arms, but they didn't. Not a single girl smiled at him and no boy but me acknowledged him. They looked at him, all right. That's all they did - stared and ogled like he was an exotic animal in a zoo.

He was exotic all right, *very* exotic for Yuccaville. Larry Jasper was the first black student to ever attend school in the Yuccaville Elementary School District.

Halfway through our morning history lesson about the Emancipation Proclamation, Principal Markham ushered Larry into room 11 and whispered something to Mrs. Regal. He then returned self-consciously to the door and ostensibly to his office, where he spent the rest of the week fielding phone calls from outraged parents and other local citizens.

"Children, this is Larry Jasper and he is our very first --." She stuck a brightly painted fingernail into her beehive and scratched. She extracted the finger and looked at it as if checking for nits. After an overlong moment of staring at her fingertip, she looked up and began again. "Larry Jasper is the first *student* of 1965 to grace our school. Welcome, Larry."

Without looking at her or anyone else, he nodded his head and stared at the floor in front of him as if he were inspecting the tile work. I don't know why Mrs. Regal expected him to say anything. Who could follow that welcome? What was he supposed to say, "It's all right, Mrs. Regal. I understand why you delivered your clumsy introduction and I want you to know that I understand and forgive you. It's perfectly understandable under these unique circumstances. You are obviously flustered by having a Negro in your classroom. Why don't you just take a five-minute break to pull yourself together in the faculty lounge while I comfort my new classmates by promising them that I will not transfer my blackness onto any part of their lily-white bodies?"

Instead, he was silenced by her speech. She finally regained a large enough portion of her senses to point out his seat, which was in the last row and farthest from the door. In fact, it was next to mine. I heard his shoes squeaking across the tile as he approached. Then, more squeaking ensued as he attempted to insert his man-sized body into a desk designed for beings smaller than most jockeys. I realized that if he wasn't trapped yet, he was approaching the need for the "Jaws of Life."

Not wanting to draw more attention to Larry (if that were possible), yet wanting to keep him from the possible ignominy of needing the janitor to disassemble his desk in order for him to not wear it to recess, I spoke up: "Mrs. Regal, in order to make Larry feel more at home, may I switch seats with him? I like sitting in back."

Since I sat in the only junior-high desk in the room and it was too big for me anyway, I was only too glad to offer.

Mrs. R was still so unsettled by her earlier lame remarks that she would've probably agreed to any suggestion at that moment. In fact, she looked relieved that I had drawn at least some attention away from her. "Sure. Why, yes. That's an excellent idea, Varrick. Thank you for the suggestion. If it's all right with you, Larry, Varrick and you may switch desks."

I turned in my seat and gave Larry a 'Well, what-do-you-think' look, but he just groaned as he seemed to not only be stuck in his desk but frozen in the pose his body had struck. Just then, the lunch bell rang and Mrs. Regal dismissed us. After the last kid left and she was locking the door, I whispered, "Need any help?"

"Yeah," Larry groaned. "Put all your weight on this thing while I try to wiggle out."

I stood on the t-shaped front leg while he imitated a snake shedding its skin. Although I was almost toppled twice, he finally escaped. Larry's legs must've had cramps because he could barely make it to the door. Mrs. Regal, whom I always suspected was a chain smoker, beckoned us impatiently. The moment Larry edged out the door she slammed it shut. Checking her watch, she murmured something about being late for something and click-clacked down the hall faster than any high-heeled person I'd ever seen.

Larry leaned against the brick wall, slid slowly to the concrete floor, and exhaled. Since his head was buried between his large knees, I couldn't make out what he'd said, but it sounded like 'thank you.' Since we hadn't formally met, I felt awkward continuing to stand over him, but I didn't want to abandon him either. I knew what it was like to be a new kid in a strange school without a single friend. So, I slid down next to him and asked, "Are you okay?"

Since his face was still buried in his stiff blue jeans, I began to worry. First, his head rocked in a nodding motion, but then it turned into a shake. He raised his head just high enough for me to see tears on his cheeks.

I was speechless. Here was a guy more mature and stronger than any student on campus, but someone who'd been profoundly affected by the reception he'd gotten from his teacher and new classmates. As I looked at his muscular body twisted to conceal his crying, I decided to give him a moment by himself. Maybe my attention to him was making him even more embarrassed.

"Hey, Larry," I heard myself say, "why don't I go to the cafeteria and get us a couple of Sidewalk Sundaes?"

He straightened, wiped his cheeks with his callused, man-sized hands, and said, "I'll join you, if that's okay."

"Okay." As I stood over him, I said, "I'd be glad to help you, but if I did we'd both wind up on the ground."

In a Southern drawl I noticed for the first time, he said, "That's okay. We've had enough attention already."

As we rounded the corner and approached the boys' room, I hesitated and said, "Hey, I'm gonna go in here for a second, if you don't mind." I was pretending I had to go, but I wanted to give my new friend a chance to wash his face before we headed for the cafeteria. He must've caught on because he followed and headed straight for the sink.

Off to the left were three boys with black hair huddled in the corner as if they were hiding something. The two biggest, whom I recognized as Bobby and Danny Krupt, were holding their cigarettes in a manner we referred to as "cupping." Bobby peered over the heads of his brothers, saw Larry and me, and said, "It's only Very Fairy."

I went over to the first urinal and pretended to go. I stared at the tile in front of me as I heard him hail Larry. "Hey you. What's your name?"

Larry was bent over the sink, splashing water onto his face. He couldn't hear Bobby, who had raised his voice slightly, "Hey, I'm talking to you, Jigaboo. What's your name?"

Danny, feeling a little bold because Larry wasn't responding to his brother, said to Bobby, "Maybe that *is* his name: Jigs, Jigs Jigaboo."

Bobby took a drag off his cigarette and laughed. "That was a good one, Danny; Jigs, Jigs what-did-you-say?"

"Jigaboo. Jigs Jigaboo."

I had finished pretending to go, so I zipped up and started heading for the door. Even though I was with the biggest kid in the school, I had no idea if he was going to stand up to Bobby. Besides, there were three of them and only one Larry. As I passed the Krupts, a hand shot out and pulled me into the smoky huddle. It was Bobby's hand. "Hey, where you going, Mister Spelling Bee?"

As I tried to answer, another hand grabbed my shirt at the chest. "He asked you a question."

My face instantly heated up. And, boy, did I feel awkward standing there on my tiptoes because of these two lifting me up by my clothes. I don't know if it was all the smoke they were generating or the situation itself, but I started feeling dizzy; so dizzy that my head began to spin. I could've puked on all three of them.

Then, a deep voice behind me sounded: "I'd leave him be if I was you."

"Oh yeah? And who would you be, big boy?"

27

Simultaneous with my being lifted, I heard the man's voice say with resonant confidence, "I would be his friend."

Danny let go of me, but Bobby still held my sleeve. The voice asserted, "Turn him loose, Boy."

Bobby did, then Larry swung me slowly around and lowered me to the floor.

I felt embarrassed by first being manhandled and then someone hoisting me like a sack of potatoes. But more importantly, I felt relieved to be delivered from the grimy Krupt Brothers.

What happened next was unfathomable, like something in a Western movie. Larry surveyed each of the Krupt boys and said, "This here's my friend. If I even hear about you messin' with him, you'll be messin' with me."

After a deafening silence, Larry pretended to poke me in the ribs with his elbow and said, "Varrick, let's get us some of that ice cream you was talkin' about."

As we stepped toward the large metal door, I felt like turning boldly and saying, "Did you hear that? You won't be messin' with either one of us from now on."

Instead, I followed Larry Jasper out that door feeling secure for the first time in two and a half years.

Chapter

5

After that fateful day when Larry Jasper confronted the Krupts and put them in their place, we became fast friends and were rarely apart.

The only exception was when I had a game or practice and Larry was home tending to his chores and taking care of his "boys," his natural brother Michael and three other foster boys in the home.

Since Larry was the oldest, Mr. and Mrs. Hicks expected him to care for the other four boys. There was Michael, age 9, and the other three - Rudy, 5; Lorenzo, 4; and Roosevelt, age 3. They were all handfuls and kept Larry constantly busy, especially the youngest whom I nicknamed 'Rosy' after the lineman for the Rams (Rosy Grier).

Not only was Rosy in need of help because of his age, he was legally blind. In addition to all that, he had a condition quite rare - he was an albino Black. Picture a little boy with light pink skin, almost white hair, and African facial characteristics and that would be Rosy.

Once I got over the initial surprise of seeing a kid like that, I accepted him. It took me two shakes to figure out he wasn't any more different than any other kid on earth. He just didn't conveniently fit into a category.

Little Rosy was actually the cutest of all the kids in the Hicks' home, including their three-year-old natural daughter Natalia, much to her consternation. If anyone pulled the limelight away from Natalia for even a moment, even someone like me whom she barely knew, she'd become furious and plot a way for the boys to get in trouble.

Natalia was a precocious three-and-a-half-year-old Mrs. and Mrs. Hicks spoiled like crazy. Her bedroom was the largest room in the house. It was painted pink (her favorite color) and featured a queen-sized bed covered by a lacy pink coverlet from France. A white antique vanity sat next to one wall, and a pink and white frilly French couch occupied the opposite wall. A dresser matching the vanity set in front of the fourth wall. Not only was her bed the largest I'd ever seen, it had a brass frame with a fancy pink canopy. Lacy curtains surrounded it on all sides.

What set off Natalia's room from all the other spoiled kids' bedrooms in America was the collection of dolls on her bed. I never counted how many she had, but there were over fifty. I don't mean store-bought dolls like Betsy-Wetsys or Barbies, but custom-made, life-like dolls that looked as if a mad scientist had frozen them. Their eyes gave you the heebie-jeebies if you looked at them for any amount of time. I always felt I was visiting a pediatric ward when I was in her bedroom.

It was Larry's job to place Natalia's dolls on the frilly sofa before she went to bed or replace them in the morning after he had made her bed. Each time, Larry had to place each doll exactly where Natalia wanted it or she'd throw a tantrum and Mrs. Hicks would run in and yell, "What's wrong? Is something wrong, baby?"

Right on cue, Natalia would collapse onto the plush pink carpet and rub her eyes with the back of her little wrists and cry, "Lah-wee's puttin' Angela (or Jolene or Megan or Annabelle) in the wrong place." To which Mrs. Hicks would glare so fiercely that even I'd have to look away. "Boy," she'd say, "you bettuh put dem dolls back propuh or I'll take a switch to your backside. I spent too much money on 'em to have you not treat 'em right. If I have to come in here again, I will not be happy, you hear me?"

Larry, who always looked very humbled, would answer, "Yes, ma'am," and then apologize to Natalia before Mrs. Hicks would be satisfied enough to return to her soap opera or the meal she was preparing for just her and Natalia.

Much of my time with Larry was spent watching him remove or replace Natalia's dolls to her liking. No one else was permitted to handle them, so I couldn't help. (I tried once and it resulted in Larry getting beat, so I never did again.) Even though Larry became my second-best friend that year, it was a chore to visit him. It took all my self-control to keep from defending him.

In all the years since '65, I've never met anyone as willful as Natalia. No telling how she eventually grew up, but I feel sorry for her husband (if she has one).

Being at Larry's wasn't completely bad, though. When he'd finished dressing and grooming the four boys and he'd made Natty's bed and placed all those dolls just so, we usually had a few minutes to shoot the breeze. If he'd been having a bad day, we wouldn't talk much at first. But, pretty soon, ol' Larry would brighten up and talk about his two greatest loves - cars and boxing.

We shared the same tastes in both, Cassius Clay being our favorite boxer and the Ford Fairlane our number-one car. Larry knew more about both than I did. When he wasn't showing me his foster father's car magazines or drawing his own designs, he'd demonstrate boxing moves in the garage. Mr. Hicks had a speed bag and a heavy bag hanging on the opposite side of the garage from where his brand-new Fairlane set when he was home.

Larry taught me some tricks about boxing. He showed me how to jab, feint, bob, weave, and even how to throw a hook with my right. Even though Larry was right-handed, he taught me to box using a left-handed stance.

On a couple of occasions, when Larry forgot to pull down the garage door, the Krupt Brothers skulked by and watched. They'd laugh or talk just loud enough for Larry to hear, but he'd never look their way. "Don't pay 'em no mind, Varrick. They don't deserve your attention."

I confessed more than once to Larry that it wasn't possible for me to forget them. He looked at me thoughtfully and seemed to understand.

"Okay. Well, when you're shadow-boxing, just pretend you're jabbin' at their faces and pretty soon, before you know it, their faces'll disappear and your anger will, too."

I figure he had had experience doing that with someone else's face in the dusty, breathless air of a garage whose walls were plastered with boxing posters.

When that happened, I'd feel a twinge of fear for Larry. Deep down, I had this omen that violence would be his undoing. But, I'd shrug it off and concentrate on his instructions; and in the midst of throwing combinations, I'd feel my fear of the Krupts evaporate. During those

31

moments, I felt free, unencumbered. Something inside me jumped for joy, the hairs on my neck stood on end, and anything seemed possible. Those moments of freedom were the highlights of my time spent with Larry. I'm not sure, however, that Larry ever felt that same freedom.

Chapter

6

I know I mentioned that my life hadn't been the same since Dad died. Truth be told, *nothing* was the same after Dad died. My family wasn't the same, including how my mother and sisters acted toward each other and me. Without Dad, my sisters pretty much ran wild. They usually did whatever they wanted, whenever they wanted. Discipline had disappeared from our home almost as soon as the funeral was over.

My older sister Deirdre became sullen and resentful toward the rest of us. In fact, whenever we were out in public, she'd pretend she wasn't with us. And when she was home, she stayed in her room, stockpiling her favorite goodies. She rarely came out unless she wanted to watch TV.

After Dad's death, my life changed too, but in a different way. When he'd been alive, change was the *only* constant in our house. One year, my father was immersed in inventing gadgets, the following year he was caught up with theater, and the year after that he'd been consumed by politics.

Of course, we kids had been expected to fall in with whatever program our father had adopted for that particular year. When he was on an invention streak, we were his apprentices. When he acted in plays, Deirdre was also forced to perform, I helped with props and Tess handed out programs. During his political campaigns, "Dee" and I placed bills on the windshields of practically every car in town and Tess helped fold some of the 4,000 he had ordered from a local printer.

After Dad was killed, these activities halted. Everything moved to the garage where it rested on his workbench. His scripts and inventions took up one side while his campaign materials occupied the other. What little Dad left behind filled our dusty garage.

Although Dad seemed to become just a memory for my sisters, he remained the centerpiece of my life. Every memory, memento, or story about him became catalogued in the scrapbooks I kept stacked on the bookcase in my bedroom. And the twenty photographs of him dominating a wall in his study remained when Mom let me use his office for my bedroom.

The biggest trouble in my life started when I retreated to my room. Since Dee shunned contact with me and holed up in her room when Mom was at work, I was on my own. I'd close my door and amuse myself. When I wasn't studying photos of Dad, reading comic books or watching a TV show or movie about ghosts or angels, I wrote about or to Dad.

Of the twenty-two scrapbooks I had compiled, eight consisted of letters from me to Dad. They detailed events at school and home followed by lists of questions about heaven. I was certain Dad had made his way past St. Peter at the pearly gates and was in heaven for eternity.

Whenever I sat in my room writing those letters, I composed them out loud. It helped me organize my thoughts and feel close to Dad. My sisters gathered by my door and eavesdropped. They reported to Mom what I was doing, but she dismissed it all as harmless. She knew that of us three kids, I had taken Dad's passing the hardest.

One blustery afternoon on Palm Sunday, I lay on my foldout couch reading the newest edition of Casper the Friendly Ghost. Playing on the black-and-white TV at the foot of my bed was the original version of "Angels in the Outfield," my favorite movie, which combined my two loves - baseball and angels.

Somewhere in the middle of reading Casper, a strange sensation that I was no longer alone in the house overtook me. In fact, I was no longer alone in my room. Something or someone was there with me. I don't know what tipped me off, but I sensed someone close by.

I had alternately been reading my comic book and watching 'Angels in the Outfield' when it struck me that the TV screen was partially obstructed. Since I was so used to Deirdre invading my privacy by perching on the edge of my bed to watch TV, I first thought it was she sitting there. But then I remembered she had joined Mom and Tess on a shopping trip and wouldn't be returning for another hour.

Too afraid to raise my head enough to see if this person was still obstructing the set, I cagily lowered the top of my comic book to spy a knee clothed in white. All I could do at that moment was focus on it. My eyes were frozen on it for the longest time, and my ears filled with the pounding of my heart.

Finally, after a long, breathless amount of time, a voice sounded. It was friendly, authoritative, and had equal parts concern and duty in it. "You didn't think we had knees, did you?" After I raised my head, it continued. "And it's only in movies and stories that we have wings. I don't know where that myth started anyway. Probably the Devil. He loves deceiving man. It's what he lives for; and according to the manual, it'll be his undoing."

I must've looked shocked because he said, "You haven't seen a ghost, Varrick; just your first angel."

He was slender, but muscular. Deirdre would've drooled over him like he was John, Paul, or George. He was matinee-idol handsome, but seemed nice, humble. He had a humility that practically put me at ease.

He pointed to the invisible angels backing up the outfielders for the Pittsburgh Pirates on TV. "The Boss would never stand for us wasting our powers catching fly balls for mortals. Not that we haven't done it in the call of duty. It just isn't His plan for us to shag fungoes. Know what I mean, Varrick?"

"How did you get in here?"

His eyes glanced upward as if to signify God's intervention, then laughed. "I've been trying to figure that out for several millennia. He always prepares a way for me, and before I can say 'Earth,' I appear where He wants."

Even though he was doing the talking, I felt we understood each other. He seemed to look inside me and know what I was thinking before I said it. Deep down inside I knew why he was here, but I needed to hear it.

"What are you doing here?"

"I have some explaining to do. But first, I better introduce myself.

35

I'm George and I'm a guardian angel."

I pinched myself and it hurt, so I was sure I wasn't dreaming. "You're *my* guardian angel? Didn't know I had one."

"Everyone has one, but I'm your father's."

"That means he's in heaven."

"Sort of. It's complicated and hard to explain to a mortal, but technically he's in heaven."

"*Technically?* What's technical about heaven?"

He rested his white-haired head onto one of his elegantly sculpted hands and pondered my question.

I was starting to not just feel comfortable, but a little cocky. "I don't mean any disrespect, but you don't seem to know what's going on. Where *is* my dad exactly?"

He resumed his 'Thinker' pose and said, "He's in a good place. You could call it heaven."

"But it's *not* heaven?"

"It's not what the manual refers to as heaven. It's not the 'bosom of Abraham.'"

"So, for two and a half years Dad has just been…"

"Well, first of all, time doesn't exist anywhere but here. And, second, he's not in a Limbo-like state."

"Where is Limbo, anyway?"

He cleared his throat. I wondered whether angels got colds. "Listen, I don't wish to be rude, but we've got to wrap this up."

"I thought you said there's no such thing as time, except on Earth. George, George? Are you still--?"

My bedroom door burst open. Deirdre smirked and tossed her head from side to side so that her brown pigtails danced. She mimicked, "George, George? Are you still there?" She straightened and her pigtails stopped their jig. "What are you doing and who is George?"

She ran to the kitchen where my mother was fixing a cup of instant coffee. "Mom, you should've heard Varrick just now. He was talking to someone named George."

She replied, "Oh? I don't think I've met George."

"Don't be stupid. He wasn't talking to anybody. The point is there wasn't *anyone* in his room."

Mom quit stirring. "Don't ever call me stupid, young lady. Hey, come back here when I'm talking to you."

Since I had already closed my door and leaned against it, Deirdre couldn't reenter. She pounded on it and taunted, "Varry Fairy, can George come out and play?" She pounded on the door again for good measure and then gave it a kick. "Jerk!" she intoned as she headed to her room.

When I was certain she wasn't coming back, I fell to my knees and prayed. I thanked God for sending George to see me and asked if he could return to help me. As I continued my petitions to God, asking Him to guide my mom and Larry Jasper, I was aware of his presence again.

"You know that's why I came, don't you?" This time he stood by the south wall admiring my dad's pictures.

"Because my sister torments me day and night?"

He laughed. "No, I mean because of your prayers."

I sat up straighter. "You listen to my prayers?"

"Not exactly. He tells me about them."

"Who? Your – uh - boss?"

"*Our* boss."

"*Our* boss? You mean, God Almighty?"

"God Almighty, Yahweh, Jehovah, The Creator of Heaven and Earth. He has many names."

"*You* talk to God?"

"Why are you so surprised? You talk to Him, too."

"Yeah, but that's different."

"Not really. He talks to everyone, but not everyone hears Him." I must have looked shocked because he said, "Close your mouth. You might catch a fly."

He sat in the same place as before and invited me to join him. Then he explained that he'd been sent to help me out with a few things. He couldn't make any guarantees, but he would do what he could to help me.

"Why?"

He looked down. "I made a big mistake two and a half years ago. I knew your dad would get hit, but I thought he'd pull through."

I had an urge to swallow, but I couldn't. It took all my resolve but I finally did. Feeling faint, I lay back on my bed and stared at the ceiling. It was all so overwhelming that I had to sort it out. It was like a dream, only real. Yet, Deirdre hadn't seen him. "How do I know you're real?"

"You can only know by believing."

I sat up. "I know! I'll touch you."

"You can't."

"You mean, you won't let me?"

"I mean you can't. Go ahead and try."

I rose up on my knees and crawled toward the bed's edge where he was perched. With my left arm I reached for him, but there was no sensation. Even though his form continued to be visible, it had no mass. "Am I imagining you?"

"No, you're seeing me all right."

"Can other people see you?"

"No."

"Then how can I?"

"Let's just say divine intervention and faith."

"Has anyone else seen you?"

"Not for a long time." He cleared his throat again. "I've got to go. The purpose of my visit is to let you know I exist and that I'll be here from time to time to offer my help. Do you have any requests?"

I knew immediately what I wanted, but I didn't want to appear eager. "Just one."

"Yes?"

I wanted to say it without crying, so I took a deep breath and swallowed. "I want to see my dad."

"I'm sorry, but you won't be able to."

"Why not?"

He looked at the ceiling. "It's never been done."

"What hasn't?"

"A person coming back to Earth after moving on."

I crossed my legs Indian-style. "What about Topper?"

"Topper? What's a topper?"

"It's a TV show and a movie about a male ghost."

George smiled sadly. "He's just a character, a figment of someone's imagination."

"What about haunted houses?"

"Varrick," he explained patiently, "ghosts are not the spirits of once-alive humans. I'll explain it to you sometime. But for now, just know that I will be here from time to time to help. Which brings me back to my question: what kind of help do you need?"

All I could think of was to ask to see Dad again, but I knew how that would go. I needed help, but I couldn't figure out exactly what I needed. After all, I was just an eleven-year-old kid. It wasn't like he was a genie and I had three wishes. "My life hasn't been the same since, since... well, you know. And my family hasn't been the same either."

He looked dumbfounded for the third time since he had appeared. He seemed uncertain as to what to do or say. Finally, he shrugged. "I hear death has a way of changing things for the ones who survive. Are you sure there isn't something I can do for you?"

"No, I guess there isn't anything you can do for me if you can't bring my dad back. I mean you can't make Bobby Krupt or my mean sister leave me alone."

As he stood there looking helpless, I felt sorry for him. He reminded me of Clarence in 'It's A Wonderful Life,' the angel who hadn't earned his wings yet.

I just shook my head and thanked him for trying to help. He said he'd be back, but he didn't sound confident.

Deirdre had resumed eavesdropping. Of course, she could only hear me. She wasn't able to hear or see George. She had heard me ask twice to see Dad. She'd also heard me get choked up and beg. She definitely heard me mention her and Bobby Krupt in the same breath. That was the mistake that started all the trouble.

She tiptoed back to the kitchen and had my Mom listen at the door, but all Mom did was shake her head sadly and whisper for Dee to leave me alone.

Mom probably thought that would be the end of that, but she didn't know Deirdre as well as I did.

Chapter

7

Kathy Regal sat in the teachers' lounge and smoked thoughtfully as she read a student's essay. She had had indications before of Varrick O'Connell's distress over his father's death, but his latest essay especially worried her. Varrick was a well-mannered, bright boy. He was the brightest student she had had in her nine years of teaching sixth grade. He had always seemed well balanced, and she had admired how he had dealt with his father's death.

So, it was with alarm that she read his newest essay. In response to the assigned topic 'The Most Unusual Thing to Ever Happen to Me,' Varrick had written about a meeting with an angel in his bedroom. He recounted in detail a conversation with his father's guardian angel followed by his older sister bursting into his room unannounced.

Although Kathy hadn't directly discussed the essay with Varrick, she *had* asked him if he understood the topic. He'd given her a stern look and replied, "Of course, Mrs. Regal. You wanted the most unusual thing to ever happen to me. That's *exactly* what I wrote about."

Kathy considered calling Mrs. O'Connell and setting up an appointment, but figured it might upset her. Marge O'Connell seemed like a vulnerable woman strapped with the burden of raising three children while working full-time at a low-paying job. The only conference they had previously had consisted of Marge requesting Varrick be held back the following year and Kathy arguing for him to be skipped to eighth grade. Marge had thought retaining him would be good for him socially since he didn't seem to have many friends, while Kathy thought he'd be better served academically by skipping a year. Throughout their meeting, Mrs. O'Connell had seemed distraught about her son.

Kathy Regal was certain that discussing Varrick's imagined chat with an angel would overwhelm Marge with worry. She considered putting the situation on hold when Cindy Bevins walked in to get her lunch from the refrigerator. Cindy was the new school psychologist who had been hired at midyear. Fresh out of college, she was full of enthusiasm and concern for her 'clients,' as she preferred to call students.

Stubbing out her cigarette and smiling at Cindy, Kathy invited her to join her. "I've got something to discuss with you, Miss Bevins, if you don't mind talking shop."

Sitting down as if a book were balanced atop her head, she said, "No, I always welcome opportunities to dialog with fellow staff members."

Kathy laughed inwardly at the woman's stiff response, but forged ahead anyway. "Good. I have a concern about one of my students. Do you know Varrick O'Connell?"

"No, I can't say I know her."

"Varrick is a *boy*. In fact, he's my brightest star."

Cindy stared at her carrot as if it might remind her of the boy. "Varrick, Varrick. What does he look like?"

"Well, let's see." She lit another Lucky Strike and tossed the match into the metal tray. Cindy pretended the acrid smoke didn't make her want to bolt from the low-ceilinged room. "Varrick O'Connell is a well groomed, blond boy with a fair complexion. He's thin, but fairly healthy."

"Does he have freckles and talks to himself a lot?"

"Yes. Do you know him?"

"We haven't talked, but I've observed him on the ball field talking to himself while playing the outfield."

Kathy exhaled a stream of smoke over Cindy's shoulder. "Well, that might be considered harmless by itself, but today I got this essay from him. I'd like you to read it."

Cindy's brow furrowed as she began reading. Knowing Kathy would watch her, she wanted to appear concerned and professional. She did a good job because Kathy spoke up. "Pretty scary, right?"

Cindy tried to sound as casual as possible. "Oh, a lot of kids have reveries." She then finished it and realized she hadn't fully digested its

41

content. She'd been so busy posing for her colleague that she hadn't absorbed the boy's writing. The second time around she realized how skillfully he wrote, especially for a sixth grader. His vocabulary was adult and he possessed a great attention to detail without being wordy. She admired his writing and wished she'd written that well when she was eleven.

When she finished, Cindy said, "He's very talented, gifted even. He's already writing like a college student. What a vivid imagination!"

Kathy frowned. "That's the problem. I didn't ask for the kids to *imagine* something. I asked them to tell me about the most unusual event to ever happen to them."

"Maybe he misunderstood the assignment."

"Unh un. He is not one to misunderstand assignments."

"He probably just ignored the topic and plowed right into a story he was dying to tell."

"First of all, Varrick O'Connell doesn't *ignore* anything. He's the most compliant kid I've ever taught. Secondly, the old movie he's talking about – 'Angels in the Outfield' – *was* on TV last Sunday afternoon. I watched it."

"I'll tell you what I'll do. I have a friend who's a psychiatrist at Napa State Hospital who specializes in this very thing. In fact, he's working on an article for the APA right now that deals with preadolescent boys who have delusional episodes. Maybe he can shed some light on this."

Kathy reached for the paper and began reading. "I'd appreciate it if you'd call Varrick in, get to know him, and see if he'll admit that this actually happened."

"Okay, but I'll need his mother's permission."

"That probably won't happen."

Cindy frowned. "Why not?"

"Mrs. O'Connell is a *very* private person. You'll be lucky if she even talks with you."

"What about the sister he writes about?"

"Deirdre? She's the opposite. She would tell a complete stranger her life story."

Cindy Bevins chewed thoughtfully for a while before stopping abruptly. "I'll call my friend and consult with him. Then, if he thinks there's anything to this, I'll talk to the boy and his family."

Kathy watched Cindy fold her bag meticulously, drop it in the trash, and prepare to leave. As she strode like the charm-school graduate she was out the door, Kathy couldn't question her own judgment in asking for her help.

◎ ◎ ◎

Cindy Bevins had never made personal calls at work, but she reasoned that the Varrick O'Connell situation was an exceptional case for breaking her self-imposed rule. After all, she was requesting assistance from a colleague who happened to be her fiancé. She locked her office door before dialing the operator. After connecting with the hospital, she paced as far as the cord allowed.

"Dr. Gayle is not in his office at the moment. I will page him if it's important. Who is calling?"

Afraid the officious woman might not page him, she played her trump card. "I am his fiancée."

Several seconds later, a thin, reedy voice came on the line. "Cindy? Is that you?"

She straightened and asked, "Paul, may I have a minute or two to consult with you about a client?"

Paul's response, like Kathy Regal's, was a struggle to keep from laughing at her formality. "Sure, Snuggles; anything for my baby. What's up?"

Her face warmed. She hated it when he patronized her. And she also hated the various nicknames he called her. But, she rallied after realizing how much he had helped her through college and her yearlong job hunt. If it weren't for Paul Gayle, she wouldn't have her job.

She launched into summarizing Varrick, his essay, and her conversation with Kathy Regal. As she described the boy's composition, Paul took notes. He sat erect and clenched his jaw as he kept up with Cindy's flow of facts and observations. When she finished, he sat back. "Well," he began, "it sounds as though this boy could be suffering from the very disorder I've been researching." Paul had been studying the significantly high incidence of boys ages seven to twelve who claimed to have seen ghosts or angels soon after the death of a significant person in their lives. What particularly fascinated Paul Gayle was that the boy was still hallucinating more than two years after his father's death.

"Cindy, this is the very case I've been hoping for."

"I know. That's why I dropped everything to call you."

"Have you interviewed him?"

"No, I need to get parent permission. His teacher doesn't think his mother will cooperate."

"Gang up on her. Get the principal and teacher to meet with you and her. Impress on her the need for professional intervention."

"But, Paul, there aren't any therapists here. Remember, I'm in the middle of the Mojave Desert."

"Good. That means she'll be open to having someone like me assess the boy. Listen, give him a simple battery of tests and then refer him to me. I've got enough in the budget to fly down and meet with him. Plus, I can see you. We'll kill two birds and mix business with pleasure, if you know what I mean. What do you think?"

Cindy's face blushed again. He'd been her mentor in so many different ways that she couldn't help but be grateful on several levels. He was her mentor, lover, therapist, father confessor, and hero. "We need to be discreet, Paul. After all, this isn't Napa Valley."

He laughed. "No, I guess not. Yuccaville sounds more like Hooterville. Listen, just get the ball rolling and I'll take care of the rest. This kid is exactly what I'm looking for. The research will write itself. Call me as soon as you get things tied up. Gotta go, Sweetie."

The line went dead and Cindy looked at the receiver as though it had offended her. She told herself he must be busy and dismissed his abruptness the way she had the other times he had hung up on her.

Chapter

8

As the season wore on, I gained confidence. The Eagles were playing good ball - our pitching was steady, defense solid, and the offense scrappy enough to win most games by a single run. We compared ourselves to the LA Dodgers. If we got a guy on base, we'd usually manage to bring him home with a combination of steals, bunts, and sacrifice hits.

After the first round, we'd won six and lost once. (The defeat was our opener against the Leviathans.) Being in undisputed second place gave us a reason to hold up our heads. We were at least better than six other teams, if not the Leviathans.

By May we'd forgotten the humiliation of our opening loss. We had put our game in order and congratulated ourselves on how nicely we'd done the job. We even said we had a chance at first place, arguing we were only a game out with two rounds left to go.

As luck would have it, the Leviathans were missing their star player when we met the second time in May. Ross Ramsey (a.k.a. "Big R") was absent. It was rumored he'd been rushed to the emergency room at Yuccaville Memorial the night before and expected to remain there a few days.

Although we were retired in order the first three innings, things began looking up in the fourth. Our leadoff man, Bunny Youngman, drag-bunted down first and reached first just before the throw from their second-string pitcher. The next guy up – Steve Sweeney – lifted a high fly to left that allowed Bunny to tag up and reach second. Jack was up next. He hunkered into his trademark slouch and fouled off eight straight pitches until he found one he liked, which he flared to right.

With one out, I felt uplifted hearing my name announced as I strode to the plate. "Center fielder, number seven, Varrick O'Connell." Swinging the bat loosely and looking at Mr. Rodriguez in the third-base box, I picked up the bunt sign. Smiling to myself about our secret strategy, I stepped into the box and dug in with my rubber spikes and assumed my Maury Wills stance. "He's gonna bunt!" I heard the third baseman yell. With every Leviathan chattering "Hey batter, hey batter, swing!" I momentarily lost my confidence and missed the pitch completely.

Stepping out of the box, I looked for my sign and saw Coach Rodriguez sticking with his plan for me to sacrifice Bunny across for our first run to break the tie.

I could tell by how the infielders leaned forward that they were fully expecting me to lay one down. I had a brainstorm! I'd pretend to swing away and hope the pitcher would throw a ball. That way they'd think we'd changed our plan and I'd bunt the next pitch so successfully that I'd actually end up on base and move our runner across.

The next pitch looked marginal from the moment the pitcher released it. I feigned a swing and was proud to see the disappointed look on his face when I didn't bunt. I smugly smiled at him and backed away from the plate when I heard the ump snarl "stee-rike two." Coach R blanched and pounded his thighs with doubled fists. "Varrick!" he lamented. "Ay, yi, yi, Panchito." He looked so disappointed that I considered running over to console him. He gazed at me with a stupefied expression before the ump yelled, "Play ball." Coach finally realized he should give me a sign. He signaled me to swing away.

I stepped back in and waggled my bat like I was summoning all the power I could. The pitcher, who'd struck me out before, threw a heater right down the pipe. I reached out and flicked the ball so it dropped like a wounded bird, dying midway between the mound and the first-base line. Time stood still as I tried to reach the bag before the infield could react. Even the runner stared with his mouth wide-open until my approach startled him into action. I sprinted past the bag with a vengeance. It seemed like I had momentarily lost my hearing from running so hard, but as I waited for the ump to motion me safe or out, I heard a huge groan from our bleacher section. As I turned to see the

46

ump give the palms-down sign I was praying for, the groan increased. I looked over at Jack on second for an explanation. He pointed glumly toward the Leviathan bullpen.

There, bigger than life, was my nemesis warming up. I felt a blow to my gut, leaned hard on my thighs and hung on for support. Despite escaping Coach's doghouse by bunting our first run over with two strikes, I was crestfallen. "That's not fair," I whimpered as I saw the rangy hurler whip one ball after another over the bullpen plate. Each crack of the catcher's mitt sent a blow to my stomach.

I don't remember the rest of the inning, except that Big R came on and threw more heat than a welding torch. Before I could spell d-i-s-a-p-p-o-i-n-t-m-e-n-t, I was jogging with Jack to our positions. We avoided talk, and I was glad. I was afraid if I uttered even a word I might bawl like a baby. I was overcome by anger, resentment, and fear. A pall had been cast over the game.

We held on to our flimsy one-run lead until the bottom of the sixth and final inning. The L's copied us by scoring a run on a bunt, fly ball, and single base hit. And then, with one out, Guess-Who came to the plate. Just like in "Casey at the Bat," a hush fell over the crowd. Ramsey towered over everyone, even the ump. But something amazing happened just then – the wind started blowing like crazy. It gusted directly toward home plate at a clip of forty miles an hour, but Big R didn't step out of the box to wait it out. He hunched over and leaned toward the mound.

With an assist to Mother Nature, our twirler threw the hardest fastball of his career. The wind grabbed and lifted it up to Big R's eyebrows. Grimacing and squinting, he swung furiously. The ball sprinted off Ramsey's bat like a bird in flight. Since it was headed straight for the center field fence, I did too. With sand pelting my face, I raced toward the low green fence. Afraid of running into it full force, I momentarily turned my back to the ball. When I was five feet away, I turned back and tried to track its flight. For a long moment I had no idea where it was. I actually remember wondering if it had exploded and disappeared into the dusty sky above me.

Craning my neck and holding my glove aloft as if that would do any good, I searched the heavens for the white pill. Then, it suddenly reappeared just above me. I flinched at its closeness, but continued hoisting my glove. As the ball whooshed by, I stabbed at it with my glove. Like a rock, it made a heavy thud on my mitt. For a split second my whole body rejoiced with glee. I caught it! I had actually caught it! But before I could clamp it with all my might, it skipped off and continued over the fence. As if it were moving in slow motion, I watched it lob lazily over the Silver Spur Coffee Shop sign and plop onto the hardpan dirt just out of my reach.

As I slumped over the fence and watched the ball roll across 20th Street, a roar exploded from the Leviathan section. People jumped up and down and hugged each other to beat the band. After a deep breath, I joined Jack for our jog to the dugout. The shocked expression on his face felt like what I must've been wearing on mine. When we reached the dugout, we patted each other's back with our gloves and gathered our gear.

The announcer's voice spoke up. "It has come to our attention that this game is under protest. Please stand by." Again, Jack's wide-mouthed disbelief matched mine. We had no choice but to give each other a shrug since we'd never heard of such a thing before. All we knew was that our coach had disappeared and some kind of review was proceeding. We heard the gruff, gravelly voice of the L's coach yell "Bull#@&*" as he ascended the stairs to the scorekeeper's roost. Since most of our teammates had already left when the announcement came over the PA, only Bunny, Jack, and I were in the dugout. We paced up and down the steps, staring at each other expectantly.

Finally, after the longest wait of my life, a second announcement was made. I'll never forget it: "After further review by both umpires and the League President, it has been ruled that the visiting team played an ineligible player and will therefore forfeit today's game. The official winner is the Yuccaville Eagles."

Bunny, who'd always been the biggest curser on the team, let loose with, "Well, s--t and Shinola, wadya think of that payola? We won. Is that boss or what?"

"Bunny Youngman, what are you doing?" It was Coach Rodriguez back from the protest meeting. He asked again, as though he were disapproving of Bunny's language. Coach, after all, was a very devout Catholic.

Bunny's mouth fell open and the wad of gum he'd been chewing fell out. I could tell it was Hubba Bubba because it was pink. "Uh…uh…I'm, uh, sorry, Coach."

Then Coach Rodriguez did something I thought him incapable of: he shamed ol' Bunny. "You geet down on your knees right now, young man, and confess."

Bunny looked at him with more than disbelief. Shock would definitely be the best word to describe it. I half expected him to tell Mr. R where he could go. But, this was 1965 and no kid on Earth had ever told a grownup where to go. He lowered down to a kneel, placed his hands in prayer position, and said with all the faux humility he could muster, "Bless me Father, for I have sinned. It has been … six months or maybe more since my last confession and these are my sins. I cursed and I ask for your forgiveness. Amen."

Coach R, as serious as could be, crouched in front of Bunny and made the sign of the cross in front of Bunny's face. "May God forgive you. Your penance is two Our Fathers and five Hail Marys."

Clearing his throat, Coach said, "Now apologize to your teammates."

Bunny said he was sorry and asked for our forgiveness, which I kind of thought was laying it on thick. Jack, however, thanked him for his apology and forgave him. I could feel my face getting really warm, so I just turned and walked to the other end of the dugout.

After being told by Coach to get up off his knees, Bunny did. And that ended one of the strangest vignettes of my young life. I had no idea it was just the beginning of many more to come. Whenever I recall that long-ago year, I think of the Forfeit Game and the "Dugout Confession."

Chapter

9

During summer break, a major part of my daily routine was visiting Betty Jo Karr. Since she lived a block from the ballpark, I went there every afternoon before practice.

Although I had a crush on Betty Jo and wanted to go steady with her, I hung out with her dad most of the time. Mr. Karr was a tall, burly man who liked kids and ping-pong, so he loved it when someone like me came over. Even though I was winless against him, I still enjoyed playing. He gave me a lot of pointers and coached me. He was really good - so good that he'd been an amateur champion as a young man.

One day while we were playing ping-pong in the Karrs' screened-in patio when I suddenly remembered something. I asked if we could stop the game for a few minutes so I could go pick up a friend. He said, "No problem. Bring him over. Your friends are always welcome." I ran out the back door and jumped on my bike. I rode three blocks to Larry Jasper's, where he was waiting in front. His foster mother wouldn't let him leave the yard unless he was with me. I thought it was a pretty strange rule, especially since Larry looked and acted like a grown-up.

"So, what do you want to do, Varrick?"

I shrugged and said, "I don't care. How 'bout we go over to Betty Jo's? We could play ping-pong."

"Okay." Larry was easy to please. Of course, you would be too if you weren't allowed to go anywhere.

Larry jumped onto the back of my banana seat and we rode rather slowly to the Karrs'. When we got there, I knocked on the front door and Betty Jo answered. She smiled at me, but her smile disappeared as soon as she saw Larry. I figured it was because he was new around the neighborhood. She left the door open and walked way ahead of us toward the back of the house. She paced around the patio until Larry and I started warming up, then she disappeared.

I soon discovered Larry was very good at table tennis. He had quick reflexes and a wicked forehand, slamming the ball past me almost every time. Before I knew it, he was whipping me 7 to 1. Since I was focused on trying to return his serve, I didn't notice Mr. Karr until he spoke.

"Well, looky here. O'Connell is getting beat badly by a..."

My mind didn't register what he was saying for two reasons. One, Mr. Karr's volume fell off as he left the room. Second, I was so intent on trying to return Larry's serve that I couldn't take in any more input at the time. However, the rest of old man Karr's sentence reentered my consciousness shortly after Betty Jo returned.

"Uh, Varrick, my dad wants to talk to you."

"Okay, be there in a minute."

"He wants to see you now." She put such emphasis on the last word that I looked up and missed Larry's next shot completely. Betty Jo – or BJ as I called her – was rarely direct and never emphatic. She didn't look like herself standing there in a demanding way. I knew something was wrong and sensed I somehow was in trouble.

"I'll be right back, Larry. Don't forget the score."

Larry laughed nervously, and then covered by sounding cocky. "I won't forget nine to one, Varrick." He laughed, then repeated the score and laughed again.

I looked back at him in mock anger and then said loudly to BJ as I passed, "Don't play with him if you know what's good for you." Betty Jo didn't respond, which I thought was weird. What was also strange was that she didn't begin talking to Larry. BJ talked to everyone. I vaguely remember being confused by this, but I figured it was unimportant compared to what Mr. Karr had to say. He must have very important news or he wouldn't interrupt a game. He knew how important the sport was and how you only interrupt someone's game under the direst of circumstances.

I arrived at the living room. Mr. Karr sat in a cream velvet chair. As I approached, he swiveled toward me, but without facing me. "Have a seat, Vee."

Since the Karr parlor was so perfect and white-glove clean, I was afraid to sit on anything and dirty it. Besides, if I sat I wouldn't be able to pace. Pacing is all I could do when I got nervous. And Mr. Karr not looking at me was really making me nervous.

"Thanks, but if you don't mind I'd like to stand."

Mr. Karr said something like 'suit yourself,' but I wasn't sure because he was rubbing his mouth with his hand. If I didn't know better, I'd say he was nervous, too.

"Varrick," he said gravely, "I've been in the escrow business for many years."

Oh good, I thought. We're going to talk business. Maybe he somehow needs advice on something related to the local real estate market.

"Varrick," he continued, "there's been an unwritten law in Yucca-ville for as long as I can remember..."

Unwritten law? I asked myself. What's that? Aren't all laws written down? Every law I'd ever known about was written down - the Constitution, classroom rules, even the Ten Commandments.

"An unwritten agreement among all local realtors that certain people aren't sold houses in Yuccaville."

What group of people? I wondered. Foreigners? People with deadly, contagious diseases? Who?

Mr. Karr sensed my bewilderment because he slowed down even more. He spoke to me firmly and patiently, like Mrs. Regal did whenever I acted up. "The group of people I'm talking about is niggers."

The word made me jump, which then caused me to feel embarrassed. I didn't want Mr. Karr to see I was a sissy about adult language, even though that word always shocked me. "Are you listening to me, young man?"

"Uh, yes sir."

"It's bad enough they're moving here by the truckload, but I'll be damned if I'll allow one in my home."

Like a puppy that doesn't get the message after his nose is first rubbed in his own mess, I tried making the connection to how this had anything to do with me. Then I remembered Larry - my friend, my protector against the Krupt brothers, and the very guy at this moment absorbing Betty Jo's stony stare. My palms sweated profusely, so I wiped them on my cutoffs. I could actually feel my feet sloshing inside my Converse sneakers as I paced.

I don't know how I was able to form words and project them loudly enough for Mr. Karr to hear me, but I did. "I'm sorry for this. I didn't want to cause a problem."

Karr made a shhhhh sound of agitation. "Hell, you're not the problem, Varrick. It's them niggers that are the problem. Just don't bring that big nigger to my house ever again, okay?"

As I answered with "Yes sir," I noted how Mr. Karr increased his volume each time he spat out the n-word. I winced each time. I was wondering if Larry could hear from two rooms away. I was itching to protect him now that I knew he was in danger. Larry was a big kid for our age, but there was no way he could defend himself against this grizzly bear of a man.

"Mr. Karr, I think my friend and I will be leaving."
He gave a slight laugh. "You got that right. You better be going. Uh, Varrick?" I was almost out of the room when I heard my name.

"Yes, sir?"

"You come back anytime. I like your style, even if you can't play a lick of table tennis." (Mr. Karr disdained the term ping-pong and always used the phrase table tennis and expected everyone – at least everyone in his home – to use the proper name, too.)

I acknowledged Mr. Karr's invitation with a nod and hurried toward the back where I found Larry staring a hole through the patio's concrete floor. Betty Jo was lounging on a chair with one calf flung over the side and the other foot resting on the deck.

I said "We better be blasting off. Bye, Betty Jo."

BJ sprang to her feet like the perky cheerleader she was and gave my arm a squeeze. She beamed her bright, wholesome smile and I knew it was going to be a long summer without her. I smiled back at her and gave a sigh that said, "What can I say?"

Without so much as a glance at Larry, Betty Jo skipped barefoot out of the patio and was gone.

Since my bike was parked on the back lawn, we were able to leave without seeing Mr. Karr. As I followed Larry out the screen door, he stopped abruptly as if he forgot something. Cupping a hand to his mouth, he yelled, "Goodbye, BJ. Thanks for the ping-pong, Mr. Karr."

The volume and timbre of Larry's voice shocked me almost as much as his use of the word ping-pong, but not near as much as the fact he actually thanked Mr. Karr.

Larry Jasper was either the most naïve or most savvy kid I'd ever known. Only the future would tell me for sure.

Chapter

10

The summer got even stranger after the episode at Betty Jo Karr's. According to Larry's foster mother we arrived back at his house two minutes after four, so she grounded him for two weeks. "One week for each minute late, Boy," she yelled at him after opening the door just long enough for him to enter. She slammed the door as if I didn't exist. I looked at my watch, which I set practically every morning to the recording on the phone. It said 3:59 p.m., one minute *before* the curfew. I knocked on the front door.

I heard Mrs. Hicks shriek, then the thump-thump-thump of her heavy body crossing the hardwood floor approached. From just behind the door, she yelled something like, "Better be the Fuller Brush Man and not your whitey boyfriend." I felt a shock of fear shoot up my legs and I almost jumped when the door opened.

To my surprise, Mrs. Hicks appeared subdued. She looked through me more than at me and was mute.

"Mrs. Hicks, I wanted to show you that we actually returned two minutes early. See my watch? It's still twenty seconds before four o'clock."

"If I want the time, I'll call the operator." This time she slammed the door.

I stood there with my mouth open because I'd been poised to tell her that my watch is very accurate as I set it almost every day to the phone recording. Unfortunately, she was gone and there was nothing I could do to set her straight.

What affected me most is what I heard next. She ranted hysterically,

"Boy, I'm groundin' you for three weeks now... Why? Cuz that smart-alecky white boy tried to put me in my place. The nerve of him..." She yelled some more, but I'd heard enough. As I stepped off the stoop, I heard a tapping noise to the right of me. Framed in the large window was Natalia, the three-year-old terror. She stood on top of a big hope chest. I had to look up at her because of the raised foundation of the house. With her little brown hands pressed against the glass and her eyes wide open, she stuck her tongue out as far as she could. I had half a mind to do something in return, but what could I do? I'd never flipped the bird at anyone in my life, and if I did then I'd never see Larry again.

◉ ◉ ◉

The next day, as I tentatively and gingerly walked past Larry's house to see if he was in his yard, the Hicks' front door opened on cue. Descending with a little difficulty was Natalia. She wore a blue and white crinoline dress and her hair was braided with matching barrettes.

She gave me a coy smile and a wave as she skipped up to me. Looking back at the house as if afraid of being caught, she handed me a piece of paper that, folded, was no larger than a half-inch by two inches. Cupping her mouth with her free hand, she whispered, "You bettah run before Mama see you." She smiled with a hint of mischief that made me wonder whether she was teasing. Since I was worried about Larry being grounded for life, I heeded her advice and ran away without looking back.

After I rounded the corner, I unfolded and read the note. It was in Larry's writing. "V, Meet me by your house tonight at 8:30. L."

Before I had a chance to refold it, I was shoved from the side so hard that I landed on the curb. When I looked up, a hand reached down to my face and demanded "Gimme that paper, punk." My hand squeezed harder and the voice emphasized, "Gimme that paper or my brother kicks your butt." I got up slowly, brushing off my backside where it had landed partly on new-mown grass and partly on concrete. I squinted at the three Krupt brothers framed by the morning sun.

Danny choked me from behind as little Tony approached. "You heard my brother. Hand over the paper, Stupid."

I didn't respond, not because I refused, but because I was paralyzed with fear. My entire body was as stiff as an ironing board, but that all changed when Tony punched me in the stomach and I dropped to the street. The paper fell out of my hand and landed a couple of feet away. Bobby reached down, picked it up, smirked, and read the note aloud in a halting manner. As if it took a great amount of brainpower to understand it, he studied the message with a grimace. Finally, he frowned harder and glared a hole right through me. "You better be there, punk."

Danny and Tony repeated their brother's command simultaneously and then laughed at their timing. I had no choice but to slink around the corner, even though I wanted to head back the way I'd come.

◎ ◉ ◎

The rest of the day was ruined because I spent it fretting about the 8:30 meeting. I was worried mostly about Larry. Even he couldn't handle the three Krupts by himself. They would lay in wait and ambush him when the time was right, and there was nothing I could do to warn him. Since they lived on his street, they could easily catch me trying to intercept him a few minutes early. I played every possible scenario through and couldn't imagine a good ending to any of them.

As the sun set and the appointed time passed, I watched from the safety of our living room. When it was pitch black and still no sign of Larry, I decided to check out the situation. Descending our porch, I crossed the driveway to the strip of lawn south of the house. I heard some rustling behind me and then three forms emerged from the thick ivy that covered the side of our garage.

"Where's your bodyguard, little man?" Bobby teased.

"Yeah, where's your nigger, O'Connor?" Danny asked.

I was about to speak when Tony spoke. "He probably told him we was comin'."

I broke protocol by acknowledging the younger kid's existence. "I did not. Why don't you shut up?"

I realized my folly. Everyone got quiet. I could barely see anything

57

now, just the Krupts' eyes and teeth shining at me in the darkness. I was about to be thrashed by a pack of wolves!

As I turned to face the two older boys, Tony shoved me from behind. "What'd you say? Did you tell me to shut up?"

I swallowed, or at least tried to. My tongue was dry and swollen, so words weren't coming easily. But I had to say something. I couldn't back down to a kid two grades behind me. How could I hold my head high at school ever again? I did the only thing any self-respecting boy could do in my situation: I repeated myself.

For the second time that day, Tony Krupt punched me in the stomach. This time it was higher and took my breath away. I doubled over and held my stomach. I suddenly felt many emotions at once – fear, fury, outrage, and shame. My eyes teared up and I fought back the urge to wipe them.

"Oh, is the little baby crying?" Tony said in a pouty, little boy way of taunting.

There is nothing more humiliating for a boy than to be bullied by a smaller kid. I knew fighting back was futile. Even if I could find the kid and beat him into submission, his two older brothers would jump in and beat *me* to a pulp.

However, I knew I had no choice. They weren't going to allow me to walk away. And if they did, I'd never hear the end of it: 'Did you hear about Varrick O'Connell? He turned tail on little Tony. What a sissy.'

As if in slow motion, I doubled my fists and flailed away at Tony. I was pushed from behind (probably Danny) and landed chin-first on the long grass. Tony pinned me and I strained to turn over. I was finally able to elbow him in the face and he gave way enough for me to roll over. I was in just as bad of a predicament as before, but I could now at least face my opponent. We wrestled and thrashed around on the grass for the longest time, but there was no budging him off me. When he increased his control by straddling me, I was doubly humiliated. His brothers yelled different tactics on how to hurt me. Since my arms hadn't been pinned, I deflected most of his blows. In my supine position I wasn't hitting back with any clout.

I was about to grab him by the chest and rock him off of me when a voice told us to break it up. No, it wasn't Larry. It was the last person

I wanted to see me in this predicament; the one person who'd forever taunt me with this memory; the person who always chided me about my defeats – my sister Deirdre.

She'd heard the commotion as she was trudging up the driveway, almost late for her nine o'clock curfew. Walking up to us, she scolded, "Stop it! Get up, Varrick."

Still pinned under my nemesis, I couldn't obey her command. So, instead, she walked over to us and tugged Tony's sleeve. "Get up!" she intoned. Tony complied, leaving me on my back staring up at her, exhausted. "Get in the house," she ordered. I didn't stop to register the utter humiliation of being 'saved' and bossed around by my sister. I just responded to the primal urge to retreat from danger.

I ran to my room and shut the door, propping my desk chair against it so I could have privacy. I collapsed on the floor and cried like I never had before, cursing my entire life. As I lay sprawled on the floor, I entreated God to help me. My father had left me, my best friends Jack and Larry might as well have left me, and my courage to stand up to the bullies of the world had left me.

I'd never spoken to God with such emotion. Usually I spoke to Him with formality and restraint, but the night had been so humiliating that I couldn't summon up any self-control. I was wrung out, exhausted, hurt beyond words. All I could do was sob and hold onto the floor so I wouldn't fall off the planet.

After I had stopped crying and my breathing had returned to normal, I had an overwhelming sensation someone was with me. It was, of course, George.

He sat on the edge of my desk, looking worried and helpless. As bad as I felt, I thought of comforting him. He said, "I'm back... to help. I just don't know where to start." He looked even more forlorn than I probably did. "You can't give up, Varrick. You have got to be strong."

His comments propelled me enough to get up and snatch two tissues from the box next to him. "'You can't give up? You must be strong?' That's your best advice?"

"Yes, it is."

I stared at him for a full minute. He finally said, "That's the best I can do under the circumstances. I have no experience at this, you know." I again just watched him, expecting him to offer more.

His helplessness began to anger me. I thought: *Angels have way more power than people. What's the purpose of having angels if they can't help us?*

"We only have limited knowledge and power. In fact, we're more limited spiritually than human beings."

But you have powers we don't have, I thought.

"You're right. We read minds and travel at the twinkling of an eye, but that's about it."

So if you can't do much, why are you here?

He cleared his throat. "These are unusual circumstances. I was surprised by your father's sudden decline and death. It caught me unprepared. I've been ordered to come help you."

"Help me?"

George nodded.

"With what?"

"Coping with life's problems."

"But, you've never lived a human life."

"You're right. I haven't."

"So how can you possibly help me?"

"Well," he said tentatively, "I'm not really sure yet, but I'll somehow figure it all out."

"Oh, great. You'll figure it all out." I could feel the heat on my face. "How many times do I have to get beat up or humiliated before you're going to figure it all out? What are you – an angel in training?"

"Varrick," he said patiently as he sat next to me, "have you heard the expression 'earning one's wings'?"

"Like Clarence the angel in 'It's a Wonderful Life'?"

"Is that a motion picture?"

"Yeah, it's one of my favorites. This old guy who's an angel is sent to keep this really good man by the name of George Bailey from jumping off a bridge."

"How did he do it?"

"You'd have to see the movie. But I guess that's not very practical since you don't exactly have the time."

"Remember, time means nothing to me."

"If you say so. Hey, when can Dad come talk to me?"

"That is not going to happen."

"Just one hour alone with him. That's all I ask."

"I'm sorry."

"*You're* sorry? How do you think *I* feel?"

Unknown to me, Deirdre was again listening at my door. She crept to the patio where my mother was rocking in the dark, which Mom did whenever she got depressed. Since my father died, she'd done lots and lots of rocking.

My mom stopped mid-rock when she heard Deirdre open the kitchen door. "What's wrong, Dee?"

Deirdre motioned for her to follow, and she did. They tiptoed on the hardwood floors to my bedroom door and listened. What they heard, of course, was me talking to George. Unfortunately, they only heard my voice. Because they hadn't been given the ability to hear angels, they assumed I was talking to myself.

"Listen," I said sharply, "if you're not going to help me, I don't want your help. Leave me alone."

My mom wanted to rap on the door and ask me what was wrong, but she stopped after thinking better of it. 'He's a lot worse than I thought,' she remarked to herself.

So, my mother turned and went to the kitchen, where she wrote herself a note to call my teacher in the morning. When Deirdre prepared to sneak back to my door, Mom said, "Leave him alone, Dee." All she could think to do was return to her place in the dark and pray.

Chapter

11

When the Joshua School secretary answered the phone at seven-thirty, she momentarily forgot that the school year was over. Out of habit, she paged Kathy Regal. When there was no immediate answer, she realized her gaffe. "I'm sorry, Mrs. O'Connell, but Mrs. Regal is not here. Can the Principal help you?"

Marjorie balked at speaking with the Principal as she didn't want him knowing about her son's state of mind. "No, but is the school psychologist there?"

"Yes, I'll put you through to Miss Bevins."

Since Cindy Bevins was an eleven-month employee, she worked the months of June and July. She had only August off, which she was desperately looking forward to.

Her first year hadn't been a roaring success. She soon discovered the Principal expected her to take charge of all testing and registration at the 1000-student school. Counseling took a back seat to bureaucratic tasks. She hadn't given up hope though. So, when she was interrupted while packing test materials to speak with the mother of a student she'd wanted to counsel, she brightened.

"Good morning, Mrs. O'Connell. How may I help you?"

Marjorie O'Connell couldn't match Cindy Bevins' perky tone, but she did her best to mask her worry. "I was wondering if someone could counsel one of my children."

"I'd love to speak to Varrick."

"How do you know he's the one who needs help?"

Cindy admitted that Kathy Regal had already referred Varrick to her and that she had informally observed him.

"Unfortunately, I didn't get around to calling you in time." She didn't want to tell Marjorie that Kathy Regal had advised her not to.

"So you can't talk with Varrick until next year?"

Restraining herself this time, Cindy paused before answering, "No, I can talk with him. In fact, I can test him and even begin counseling. What's your concern?"

Marjorie said she'd rather not discuss it over the phone and asked if she could drop by sometime that morning.

"Drop by anytime. I'll be here most of the summer." She'd wanted to say, 'Take all the time you want. I'll do *anything* to get away from these stupid diagnostic tests.'

The women agreed to meet at eleven.

Miss Bevins thanked Marjorie for calling, not realizing how gleeful she had sounded. Smiling at the stacks of tests in front of her, she said, "You guys will have to wait. I've got more important work to do."

◎ ⊙ ◎

Since Marjorie was the office manager at the water district, she didn't have to tell anyone about her 'early lunch.' However, she did let everyone in the office know she'd be gone early without explaining why.

Five minutes later, Marge O'Connell arrived at Joshua School. Her escort, the school custodian, knew exactly where their destination was. The year before it had been his supply closet. Since the school was pinched for space, the principal made it the new psychologist's office. It would hold all testing supplies. He never stopped to consider the effect its dark, damp interior might have on students. School counseling wouldn't gain respect for another decade. To cheer up her office, Cindy left the door ajar and brewed a pot of tea. Although Marge disliked tea, she accepted a cup when she arrived. They sat sipping and smiling at each other until Cindy broke the ice.

"How can I help you with your son?"

Marge set her cup aside. "Varrick has been overheard having conversations with an angel."

"Oh," Cindy's eyes widened until she remembered to mask her reactions. "What kind of an angel?"

Although Marge was struck by the stupidity of the question, she did her best to humor the first psychologist she'd ever met. "I really don't know what kind, but I believe it was just a reverie. You see, Miss Bevins, Varrick loves to talk and read about angels and ghosts." Cindy Bevins took copious notes in shorthand for half an hour. She wondered what her boyfriend Paul Gayle would make of all this.

After Marge told everything she could think of regarding her son, she waited for Cindy to reply. "Would tomorrow be too soon for us to meet? I'd like to get started as soon as possible."

Marge was almost taken aback by the young woman's eagerness, but it did please her that Varrick would be getting free, quick help. Now she just had to convince him he needed it.

⊚ ⊙ ⊚

When Marge pulled into her driveway after work, she was greeted by Varrick, who ran the length of Marina Street to tell her the news. "I'm going to be on the radio, Mom."

Before she could enter the house, he had told her the Eagles were playing the Leviathans for first place on Saturday. The game would be the first-ever broadcast of a Little League game on Yuccaville's only station. "Who knows, Mom? Maybe a big-league scout will hear the game and want to sign me with the Yankees."

After dinner, when he'd started winding down, Marge broke the news. Varrick reacted as though it were the most normal thing in the world – a boy being tested by the school psychologist during vacation. "As long as it's not during practice," he said before skipping off to bed.

⊚ ⊙ ⊚

Cindy was still feeling the afterglow of speaking with Paul Gayle on the phone when she heard a soft knock on her thick, metal door. Varrick had arrived early for their nine-thirty appointment. The buildings' shadows had receded from the asphalt playground an hour before and heat waves already squiggled skyward. Varrick parked his bike next to the blue door before knocking.

A head barely higher than his emerged from the semi-darkness behind the door and greeted him. "Come in, Varrick. It's nice and cool in here."

"Will it be okay if I park my bike in your office?"

Eager to start off on the right foot with her 'client,' she quickly complied: "Sure, park it anywhere."

After they exchanged pleasantries, Cindy gave Varrick an hour-long IQ test. He sat upright and, except for an occasional hesitation, worked very quickly. When the written portion had been completed, Cindy laid a series of colored geometric blocks on the table between them and timed his responses with a stopwatch.

When the IQ tests had been completed, Cindy straightened and smiled. "Well, I'll bet you're very tired. Would you like to take a break, Varrick?" He smiled and said he'd like to continue. *I've never known a child so bright and cooperative*, she thought. She then administered a Rorschach test. His answers were imaginative and full of detail and he seemed to enjoy the opportunity to tell stories. Cindy couldn't help notice that many of his interpretations were of a spiritual tone, and four of his twenty-four responses were about angels or ghosts. She took detailed notes on a legal-sized notepad, which was not standard procedure for this specific battery. Paul Gayle, however, would be angry if she didn't record everything. Sometimes she got so far behind that Varrick had to wait for her before going on to the next section.

When the psychological battery was completed, Cindy glanced at her watch and was surprised at the time. "Well, you're probably very hungry. It's noon and I haven't given you a break yet."

Varrick smiled and said, "That's okay. I'm having fun. What's next, Miss Bevins?" Cindy thought: This *is* fun. This kid is so cute and nice. And look at that smile. What a charmer! I hope Paul and I will have a boy... Whoa! Slow down, Cindy. You've only seen this kid once and you're already counter-transferring. What would Paul think?

Cindy focused on the boy's little arms and gaunt face and felt a motherly twinge. "Would you like something to eat, Honey? Maybe a peanut-butter cookie and an orange?"He grinned from ear to ear. "Sure!

65

Peanut-butter cookies are my favorite."

"Great. I'll just ask a few questions while we eat. Is that okay?" As he responded with enthusiastic nods, Cindy chastised herself for introducing food to the session. *Paul would have a fit if he saw this. He'd say I'm tainting the scientific process and confusing the therapist-client relationship by sharing food. Oh well. What I don't tell him won't hurt him.*

◎ ◎ ◎

Varrick was so excited Saturday morning that he barely touched the breakfast he usually had no trouble finishing. Marjorie even had to remind him to take his cap as he raced out the front door. "Good luck," she yelled as he ran out a second time. Since the game was still an hour away, she thought she had plenty of time to get ready. However, she hadn't planned on receiving a phone call that would make her late for the game.

It was the counselor from the school. She discussed the 'preliminary findings' of the testing and wanted to know if she could observe Varrick over the weekend.

"Doing what?" Marge wanted to know.

"I'd like to observe him in his normal activities."

"Well, he's got a baseball game at noon today."

"Oh, that would be perfect. Do you mind if we sit together?"

"Why, no. Varrick will think you're taking an interest in him." Cindy paused. "Is that good?"

Laughter sounded on the other end. "You don't know Varrick. He loves attention, *any* attention."

Chapter

12

In their previous two games, the Eagles and their rivals, the Leviathans, hadn't played to more than forty people. Saturday, however, was quite different.

The Leviathans' section was packed. With twenty latecomers forced to stand, the Ls' fans numbered more than one hundred.

Amazingly, the Eagles' count was much more than that. They not only filled up the larger home bleachers, but lounge chairs and picnic blankets were spread as far away as the first-base foul pole.

If that wasn't enough, radio station KUPI – 'Kewpie' as most people called it – broadcast the game from the ground level of the two-story scorekeeper's tower. A white banner embroidered with the station's call letters in gold hung from the window directly behind the backstop. People were so thrilled to have the game broadcasted that neither team complained about the white background distracting both teams' pitchers and center fielders.

Since it was late June and game time was noon, the weather was extremely dry and hot. Many of the spectators' nerves were tense, partly due to the heat and partly because of the firecrackers and cherry bombs going off below and around the stands. Not only were the blasts agitating, the danger of fire was uttermost in most adults' minds. Whenever a pop sounded, the bleacher-bound spectators would twist and turn toward the fields of sagebrush surrounding the diamond and hope someone hadn't been foolish enough to ignite fireworks in the desert.

After the Pledge of Allegiance was led by test pilot Chuck Yeager, the National Anthem was sung by Louise Ramsey, mother of Leviathan pitcher Ross Ramsey, who played the lead in the local production of 'Madame Butterfly.'

When Varrick ran to his position, he did so alone. Jack Bryant, his best friend and fellow outfielder, had been admitted to Yuccaville Memorial the night before. No one outside of his parents knew what ailed him. There were plenty of rumors, but none were correct. If anyone had guessed his condition, they would have had much to worry about. However, Jack's only request of his parents had been that they not tell anyone he had leukemia.

As Varrick tossed the warm-up ball to the other outfielders, he heard someone yell his name. Standing on the dugout top step and waving for Varrick to join him was Coach Rodriguez. An ache in his stomach began as he assumed he was being taken out before the game had even begun. Being the compliant kid he was, he didn't hesitate when he saw Coach's signal, but ran to meet him at first base.

"Yes sir?" he asked, desperately hoping the obvious was not about to happen. (He really couldn't blame his coach, though, since he hadn't hit Big R in two seasons.)

"Varrick, I need to move you to third base. Bunny has missed every ground ball I've hit him. You're the best glove man we have and I don't want to lose because of grounders going through Bunny's shaking legs."

Varrick sneaked a peek at Bunny Youngman, who was living up to his name. He looked as scared as any rabbit frozen in the high beams of an oncoming auto. Varrick took pity on him *and* Coach Rodriguez. He didn't have the nerve to tell him that a lefty had no business playing third, especially when he had no previous experience at the "hot corner," not to mention that this was the most important game in the Eagles' history.

"Sure, Coach. No problem."

"That a boy. Hey, Ump. Can my new third baseman get some warm-ups?"

As Varrick took several grounders from the Eagle catcher, he heard cracks about him being brought in to play third, mainly from the Eagles' cheering section. Several fathers and older brothers made disparaging remarks about Coach Rodriguez' judgment. 'Ridiculous' and 'stupid'

68

could be heard near the infield.

Varrick didn't miss any of the seven practice grounders, but he did make a couple throws that forced the first baseman to stretch. Wiping both hands on his gray flannel knickers before putting on his glove again, he motioned to the umpire that he was ready. His name was announced over the PA system and he heard it again from the many radios tuned to KUPI. The phrase 'unusual move by the Eagle manager' resounded from the transistor radios stationed among the crowd. Varrick told himself fame always had its price. He'd remembered his father stating that platitude once and now it seemed to apply.

Luckily, the Leviathans were retired in order in the first and nothing was hit his way. When he returned to the dugout, he learned of a second surprising lineup change: he'd been moved up in the batting order to leadoff. "Bunny's nerves just can't handle the pressure," Coach explained. "You, Amigo, are made of stronger stuff."

Yeah, I won't look as scared when I strike out three straight times, he told himself as he shuffled toward home plate.

Big R seemed taller than ever to Varrick. *He's grown an inch or two since summer started*, he marveled.

Ramsey stared and shook his head twice before throwing a blazing waist-high fastball that Varrick could only stare at. "That's okay, that's okay," Rodriguez yelled from the third base coaching box. "Always watch the first peetch, Amigo." There were a few titters from the Eagles fans, and Bunny's father loudly mimicked the coach.

The next two pitches were just outside and the fourth was in the dirt. He felt an emotion new to him in all of his previous at-bats against Big R – hope; hope that he might actually reach base against the toughest pitcher in the league. The feeling was short-lived, though, as the next pitch was a wicked curve that arced across the outside corner for strike two.

Backing out of the box, he foolishly looked for a sign. Coach naturally gave the 'swing away' signal by tugging at his ear. With the count full, Varrick said a quick prayer that Big R not humiliate him. As the white pill streaked his way, he swung with all his might and actually made contact, which was a miracle considering he'd shut his eyes after Ramsey released the ball.

Although the hard plunk on the fat part of the bat felt great, his heart sank when he saw a high foul drop harmlessly twenty feet behind the Leviathan bench.

Oblivious to the goings-on around him, including the play-by-play commentary delivered directly behind by a man attempting to impersonate the inimitable Dodger announcer Vin Scully, all Varrick could allow his senses to take in was the sight of the hulking, frowning mass of pitching fury looming above him.

The next windup was like every other he'd seen in his two seasons facing Big R with one exception. He saw a slight hesitation in Ramsey's shoulder area just before release. He figured in a split-second that the pause would cause him to throw high. It was just a hunch, but it proved to be correct. "Ball four," the umpire bellowed.

"Well, go ahead, Amigo. Take first," Mr. Rodriguez urged. Varrick was so shocked at drawing a walk that he actually needed Coach R's direction to move.

Little League rules are different from most levels of baseball. For example, taking a lead from any base isn't allowed and stealing is not permitted if the pitcher is standing on the rubber. The rulebook, however, *does* allow the base runner to advance if the pitcher hasn't yet stepped onto the rubber or if the ball has crossed home.

Varrick had learned of the rule by reading the rulebook. It suddenly occurred to him that he could help his team's chances by stealing second even though Rodriguez hadn't given him the 'green light.'

He stared at Ross Ramsey through eyes squinted almost shut because of the intense glare. He watched his opponent like a hawk; looking to discover every clue, however minute, of how long Big R would take to get his sign from the pudgy catcher called Fatso. Ramsey would often shake off at least the first sign and insist on another. Varrick noticed Ross had no awareness of him as a base runner. Since there was no threat of a steal while he stood on the rubber, there was no need to go into a stretch. *I'll bet he doesn't know the rule*, Varrick thought as he watched Big R even the count.

He spread his legs as far apart as his bent knees allowed and mentally rehearsed the sprint to second and subsequent slide. Sucking in a big breath and exhaling it completely, he took off a split second before Big

R stepped forward. The wind rushing into Varrick's ears kept him from hearing anything but his own breathing. Nine feet from the bag he threw his right leg forward and leaned left. His left knee scraped the hard-as-rock path and absorbed most of the friction. A sharp pain stabbed him, but was quickly forgotten when he stood to wipe off his trousers. The base ump ran over in protest before screwing his face upward and referring to the rulebook inside his head. With upraised eyebrows he said "safe" as if it were a question.

The Leviathan shortstop gasped and began to plead, but the ump hushed him by barking, "I *said* he's safe."

The L's manager climbed out of the dugout and yelled, "Hey, what the hell…" but realized the impropriety of cursing during a Little League game in the mid-1960s.

Varrick didn't dare look at Coach Rodriguez, but he could tell he was gesturing with both palms down to communicate he didn't want a recurrence of what had just transpired. So, Varrick did something he'd never done before: he ignored an adult's command. He was certain he could pull off another steal now that he had Big R's timing down. Besides, the right-handed batter shielded Fatso from making a strong throw to third.

On the first pitch, he took off like a shot. Varrick had no choice but to slide hard and his left knee again twanged in pain. He couldn't attend to it because Big R's throw sailed over the third baseman's glove. Stumbling for several feet, his feet finally untangled and he raced home. Unfortunately, he again was forced to slide.

There was an audible gasp from the crowd, and he figured the fans were as amazed as Big R. Before Varrick had a chance to wipe off his pants, both managers and two umpires surrounded him. They all yelled at each other simultaneously, as if anticipating each other's arguments.

Only the four men were yelling. The players knew not to get involved and the crowd had something else to focus on. After much frantic pointing and waving and four sets of enlarged neck veins, the home plate umpire restored order by yelling, "The runner's safe."

Coach Rodriguez gently grabbed Varrick by his uniform and was about to say "Come on," when he let out a gasp. "Oh my gosh. Your

71

leg." Varrick's left pant leg from the bottom of the knee to the hem was soaked with a bright liquid that he slowly realized was blood.

"How did that get there?" Varrick wondered as he followed the Eagle skipper to the dugout. Once he realized whose blood it was, both of his knees buckled, but Coach's grip strengthened as he toted him like a sack of potatoes.

"Mijo, get my first-aid kit," he yelled to Louie, his son and assistant coach. "Ay, yi, yi, compadre. What did you do to yourself? Your mother is going to keel me; right after she keels you." He continued scolding and tongue clucking until he had the bloody wound cleaned and dressed.

At the mention of his mother, Varrick felt a second wave of nausea. However, the one-nothing tally on the scoreboard gave him an adrenaline rush better than smelling salts and he was ready to carry on.

He figured the Eagles must have made a third out because teammates were grabbing gloves and heading for the field. Bunny Youngman, however, stared at him with both admiration and terror. "Is he going to the hospital, Coach?"

Rodriguez couldn't respond because the umpire approached and asked, "Any lineup changes?"

Rodriguez turned to check him out from head to shin. He said, "It's up to him, Ump. What do you say, O'Connell?"

Varrick brightened. "To quote a great man: 'We are made of stronger stuff.' I have to finish the game."

With that, he tried limping as little as possible out to third and shagged some warm-up grounders. Little did he know that at that very moment one of the few listeners to the KUPI broadcast was bouncing up and down on a hospital bed, ignoring the nurses' requests to stop.

◉ ⊙ ◎

Marge O'Connell was chatting with Mrs. Youngman at the snack bar when Cindy Bevins ran up. "I think you better hurry. Varrick's hurt." As they sprinted to the middle playing field, Cindy told Marge what she knew: Varrick had scraped his leg sliding three times.

When they arrived at the corner of the dugout, Marge was loaded for bear, and Carlos Rodriguez was the only target in sight. She descended the steps and approached him with uncharacteristic speed. "Why on earth did you make him slide three times? Where is he? *How* is he?"

Rodriguez simply pointed to third where Varrick leaned on both knees with his elbows and chattered with his teammates, "Hey, batter batter, Hey, batter batter…swing!"

Marge blanched when she spied the large stain on his knee, but relaxed slightly when she saw him smile and wave. She looked at Cindy Bevins for validation and got a reassuring nod. Realizing how out of place she was in a dugout of uniformed males yelling and spitting, Marge thanked Rodriguez for his first-aid assistance and excused herself.

When she arrived at the Eagles' bleacher section, she was given a hero's mother's welcome. She heard several versions of what had happened moments before and how brave her son had been. She smiled nervously and watched the game, pretending not to stare at the skinny boy in the stained uniform who hadn't looked this happy since his father had been alive.

Chapter 1

Jack Bryant's parents Paul and Dorene were eating in the commissary when the nurse approached them. "Your son is getting too emotional listening to some ball game. First he was almost in tears worrying about a certain player, and then he bounced up and down so badly I thought he'd fall out of bed. We will have to restrain him."

Paul Bryant let out a long, deep laugh that resonated through the dining room. The nurse receded three steps, spun on her heel, and exited at a jog.

"What on earth are you laughing at?" Dorene asked.

"Our only child is dying of a disease we can't even spell and the one rare moment of joy he has listening to his team on the radio is reported to us by an old bird as if he's just committed a felony or something. You don't think that's funny?"

"Well, you frightened the poor thing with that maniacal cackle of yours. I'd be afraid too if I were her."

"Well, I thank the Good Lord you're *not* her. Give me a smooch before we go back in to see our pride and joy."

Paul and Dorene walked arm in arm to their son's room where he was scheduled to receive the first in a series of blood transfusions. First for that summer, that is. All told, there had been over twenty transfusions since he'd been diagnosed with AMM (agnogenic myeloid metaplasia) at age four. The introduction of healthy blood with normal red blood cells was the doctors' only hope of stemming the leukemia. Bone marrow transplants and interferon injections were mere concepts on a researcher's drawing table, years away from becoming a reality for kids like Jack Bryant.

The second, third, and fourth innings came and went more uneventfully than the bottom of the first. The Eagles' pitcher was able to keep the Leviathans at bay, giving up two base hits and a walk. The underdogs, on the other hand, continued to be no-hit by Ross Ramsey. He retired every batter in order since Varrick's walk and run in the first.

It was the fifth inning that wrought havoc for Varrick's team. With one out, the Leviathans managed a walk and two bunt singles to load the bases. Big R, their cleanup hitter, swaggered to the plate and smiled with gritted teeth at the Eagles' dugout. Without checking for a sign from his coach, he stepped into the box and waggled his bat. Since the bases were loaded, there was no way he'd be walked intentionally. Still, the pitcher tried his best not to give him anything good. But, with the count full, he grooved one right down the middle. Big R nailed it so hard no player or spectator could follow it.

The ball rocketed off his 34-ounce bat and shot down the third base line. Being a lefty, Varrick's glove hand was nearest the line. Even then, he barely got webbing on the ball, which continued almost unabated on a straight shot four feet off the ground until finally striking the grass somewhere before the short fence and bouncing over for a ground-rule double. The next two Leviathans were retired, but the damage was done. The lead, game, and first place were all lost in one swing. The L's led 2 to 1.

Varrick tried rallying his teammates, but they were demoralized. They sat in silence, slumped against the concrete walls as if they were the ones laying in a hospital with death a breath away. The fifth was even worse than the previous three frames. Big R struck the side out in the minimum number of pitches possible - nine.

It was a moral victory for the Eagles that the Leviathans didn't score any runs in the top of the sixth and last inning, but they did manage to load the bases. The line score read: Leviathans – 2 runs, 8 hits, and no errors, Eagles – 1 run, no hits, and no errors.

When the first two batters went in six straight pitches to open the bottom half of the sixth, the door was all but closed. There wasn't an Eagle on the bench who thought they had a prayer, but the next batter – Varrick - did. Resting on his good knee, he said a quick prayer as his name was announced.

Coach R gave the bunt sign, very unorthodox for this situation. *He probably thinks I can't hit this guy,* Varrick thought as he settled in. Waggling his bat over the plate before Ramsey had even stepped on the rubber, he did everything he could to unsettle him. The first and third basemen took a couple steps toward the plate just in case he dare lay one down. The first pitch was an eighty-mile-an-hour fastball that collided with his outstretched bat. The ricochet hit the ump square on the mask, knocking him flat.

Both managers ran to home plate and joined the other umpire in staring down at the startled and stunned man in black. After being dusted off by the other umpire and given a cup of cold water, he gamely resumed his position.

Varrick crouched even closer to the plate and awaited the second pitch. The curveball arced so much it was a foot behind him before it broke. Even then it was a foot inside and he had to fall backward to escape it. Ramsey laughed as he watched Varrick lying on his back.

Coach R still gave the bunt sign, so he dug in as much as he had before. A sidearm fastball slashed across the plate for strike two. The bunt sign was now obviously off, so he had to swing away. Varrick crowded the plate so that both feet rested on the inside line. Big R noticed and bit his lip vengefully right before winding up. The sidearm heat headed right for the batter and he had no choice but to brace himself and hope the ball wouldn't break a bone. It hit the fleshy part of his right arm and caromed all the way to the dugout. The entire crowd gasped, and then the Eagles' side heartily booed Big R.

Varrick remained standing in the box with his bat still gripped in both hands. Even after the ump yelled, "Take first base," he stood still as a statue. He knew that when he let go of the bat the pain would double in intensity. When he lowered his arms, he almost jumped. He finally dropped the bat and trotted to first, still not loosening his arm completely. Coach R called time out and walked over. Varrick refused to do two things - touch the spot or look in his mother's direction.

Because of all the fuss over being hit, he knew he had a chance at stealing second. In order to do that he'd have to use both arms. As Coach talked to him he stretched both arms and tried shaking out the stiffness.

"Whatever you do, amigo, don't rub it. We can't ever show the enemy they've hurt us." Coach patted him on the back before trotting back to third. As usual, some of the Eagles' fathers yelled names at Coach as he resumed his position. Varrick realized his coach's words were directed at himself as much as they were toward his third baseman.

After the first pitch, Varrick waited for Ramsey to drop the ball into his glove, and he was gone. Above the sound of rushing wind he could hear someone yelling Ramsey's name. By the time Big R reacted, Varrick slid safely into second. The pain in his leg was only surpassed by the throbbing in his right shoulder. Coach was laughing and clapping, so he knew he'd done right.

He decided to wait two pitches before trying to steal third, and was glad he did. Bunny walked on four straight pitches, which meant the winning run was now on base. The next batter, Raul Rodriguez, was not only the best Eagle hitter, but also Coach's son. He was the only player in the league to have any success off Big R - two singles in two seasons. Things were looking as good as they ever had. Even though they'd been no-hit, the Eagles had two runners on. If Raul could hit it out of the infield, they could tie and force the game into extra innings.

The Leviathans' coach called time and trotted out to talk with Big R, who shook his head before eventually relenting to whatever the coach had ordered. After the old man disappeared into the dugout, the Ls' catcher stood and pointed his right arm toward first. Ramsey tossed a pitch three feet outside and the Eagles let out a collective sigh of awe.

Big R was intentionally walking the first batter of his career.
Raul just glared at Ross the first couple of pitches. However, right before the third pitch he said something derogatory and Big R said something back. He then reared back and threw as hard as he could toward Raul's head. Rodriguez ducked and the ball hit the base of the backstop. Varrick raced for third, rounded the bag, and headed for home. Big R fielded the rebound in front of the mound and ran toward home, too. The crowd was on its feet and the radio announcer followed suit, yelling into his mike as if it were the climax of the seventh game of the World Series. About seven feet away, Varrick dove headfirst for the plate.

Holding the ball in his gloved right hand, Big R did too. The two dirt clouds merged into one enormous mushroom. The ump stayed in posi-

77

tion and watched from behind the plate.

Varrick's hands slid over the plate before he felt Big R's mitt scrape his forearms. However, dirt flew into his eyes and mouth, causing him to choke. The umpire waited for the dust to settle. Everyone screamed his opinion of whether the runner was out. The ump was so blinded by the dust that he asked Varrick, "Did he tag you?"

Partly because of the dirt he'd swallowed and partly because of the unexpected miracle that the ump would ask him, Varrick was too stunned to speak.

"Of course I tagged him, ump. He was out. Easy."

By then, both teams' coaches had made it to the scene and were jawing first with the ump and then with each other. Bedlam reigned. The ump held up both hands and everyone quieted down. He crouched down to where Varrick still lay and asked him pointedly: "Did he tag you or not?"

The boy looked up at the ump and then a little higher at Big R, who was mouthing the words "I'll kick you're a--" behind the umpire's back. Varrick's stomach suddenly hurt the way it did when Danielle had pulled Danny Krupt off him and humiliated him. He tried swallowing but dirt was still lodged in his throat. Peering a second time at Big R who was still mouthing his threat, Varrick did what came easiest under the circumstances - he shrugged. The umpire, unaware of Big R's mouthed threats, raised his right fist in the air and yelled "He's out."

Varrick dropped his head and lay facedown at home until Coach R tugged gently on his elbow. Varrick turned over and let Coach lift him to his feet. As he limped toward the dugout and watched the Leviathans celebrating their victory, he heard Coach gasp: "Que lastima, amigo. It's bleeding again. Your mother weel keel us both."

Sure enough, the knee had begun bleeding again and the dressing had been ripped away by the slide. When he reached the dugout, Varrick slumped onto the concrete slab and winced at the pain. "You're going to need stitches, amigo. You shouldn't have slid again." He realized he might be sounding as if he were chastising his player for his heroic efforts, because he capitulated. "Don't get me wrong, Compadre. You did everything you could to win, and we are all grateful, but look at your knee."

Blood streamed everywhere, rivulets of red coursing in all direc-
tions. Coach took a handkerchief from his pocket and blotted the wound
gently. With a wad of paper towels Raul had gotten from the restroom,
Coach sopped up what he could. He used the remainder of the first aid
kit's contents to bandage the wound, which had been ripped open to a
seven-by-two-inch gaping tear.

Marge O'Connell had watched the entire process from a distance of
several feet, but had been too terrified to speak. She'd been rendered
speechless by the profuse amount of blood and reeled from the nausea.
When Carlos hoisted Varrick and turned to carry him out, he saw her.
"He's going to be all right. We just need to get him to a doctor."

She blotted her forehead with a Kleenex and said tentatively, "I guess
I can take him in my car."

Coach thought of her almost-new Chevy Impala being stained by
blood. "If it's okay with you, Mees O'Connell, I'll take him in my truck.
He'll be comfortable in the camper. You can either follow or join us."

She agreed to follow. She gave her son her 'I'm-very-worried-about-
you-but-I-don't-want-you-to-be-worried' look and patted him on the
arm. As she watched Coach load him into his camper, Cindy Bevins
approached. "I know this isn't exactly the time or the place to talk about
this, Mrs. O'Connell, but do you still want me to meet with Varrick this
week?"

She nodded before finally saying, "I'm more worried about his phys-
ical well-being now than anything else."

Miss Bevins said she understood. She watched Marge hurry to her
car and drive out of the dirt lot before she returned to writing in her
notepad.

Chapter

14

At Yuccaville Memorial, Varrick hopped on his good leg from the parking lot to the emergency room as Raul and Coach Rodriguez assisted him. Marge parked alongside the old truck and followed the three into the waiting room.

Within twenty-five minutes, Varrick had been seen by the emergency resident. Only ten stitches were required to close the gash, but the boy thought it was a major surgical procedure. He was told by the doctor to avoid any strenuous activity, especially sliding, for two weeks.

As he hobbled out the back door, Varrick stopped suddenly. "Hey, Mom, isn't Jack around here somewhere?"

Marge hesitated. "He probably is, but I'm sure he doesn't want to be bothered."

Varrick wasn't to be discouraged so easily. "Bothered? I'm his best friend. I wouldn't be bothering him."

"But how would we find out where he is?"

"Simple, Mom. We go to the front desk and ask."

The volunteer at the front desk told them that Jack Bryant wasn't seeing any guests outside of his immediate family. Just then, Varrick spotted the Bryants entering the waiting room. He waved and then introduced them to his mother.

"How's Jack doing?" the boy asked.

Mr. Bryant gave Varrick's uniform the once-over. "He's probably doing better than you are. At least he isn't bleeding all over creation. What happened to you?"

Varrick appraised his knee. "I slid sort of hard a few times. Hey, guess what? We almost beat the Leviathans."

Mrs. Bryant spoke. "Yes, we know. Jack was listening on the radio. He got so worked up we thought he was going to run out and join you at the ballpark."

"We sure could've used him." Varrick looked first at Mrs. Bryant and then at Mr. Bryant. "Do you think I could visit him?"

The Bryants looked at one another. Mr. Bryant chuckled. "Sure, why not? He's resting quietly, but if he doesn't get too riled up, I guess it would be all right."

◉ ◉ ◉

Varrick tiptoed into Room 102 and approached the lone bed. Since the blinds were drawn, the room was dim. After a minute or so, Varrick could see every feature of his friend's face as he lay sleeping. His gaunt, pale face looked peaceful, angelic even. *Now that's how I always pictured an angel would look – like Jack. George looks about as much like an angel as I look like Rock Hudson.* He could make out Jack's chart hanging on the wall above his bed. Checking to see if anyone was watching, Varrick pulled the clipboard off its wooden peg and read it:

John Paul Bryant. Height: 4ft. 10 in. Weight: 89 lbs. Condition: Critical. Diagnosis: Agnogenic Myeloid Metaplasia (Leukemia). Prognosis: Poor.

Varrick scraped the wall with the clipboard as he tried replacing it. A muffled voice asked, "Mom, Dad?"

Varrick tried to respond, but the words wouldn't come.

Jack's eyes widened as he recognized his friend. "Hey, Varry. How are ye?"

Varrick laughed. Even in the throes of whatever this was, Jack still had his faculties. He always called Varrick 'Varry' and usually followed it with the rhyming question. It was one of their inside jokes. Varrick knew he had to respond in kind. "Fine, and how are ye, Jackie me boy?" Since they were both Irish, they enjoyed using brogue accents with each other.

Jack suddenly became serious. "Hey, that was quite a game. We got robbed at the end though."

"Yeah. It was a lousy call. The ump just guessed."

"You mean - you *were* safe?"

"Is the Pope Catholic?"

"Last time I checked. Does a bear poop in the woods?"

"Of course, Silly."

"Are all bears Catholic?"

"Yes they are, but just barely."

Varrick was on the verge of busting up, but he remembered the sober circumstances and swallowed back his laughter. A lump formed in his throat almost instantly and he almost wished he hadn't laughed after all.

"So, let me see the damage, Mr. Third Baseman."

Varrick dragged a chair to the bedside to prop his leg on and pulled up his uniform to reveal the bandage. Jack said with mock impatience: "Well, pull the sucker off and show me. The radio guy called it 'a bloody gash.'"

When Varrick slowly pulled back the dressing, Jack raised up to get a better look. "Ouch," he said.

Varrick replaced it gingerly and exhaled.

"Does it hurt, Varry?"

"Is the Pope Catholic?"

"It depends. Is he a bear?"

"Of course, Silly. All Catholics are bare sometimes."

They both broke up. After they'd giggled awhile, there was silence. For the first time in their lives, they were confronted with the inadequacy of words. Jack held his hand out to Varrick, who responded with a handshake. Jack instead clutched his hand. Varrick felt embarrassed for a second, but then surrendered to the gravity of the moment. Here he was holding a boy's hand for the first time in his life. He noticed how cool and almost lifeless it felt. *So is this what death feels like?* He asked himself. They held hands for a long time. Varrick eventually sat in the chair and kept holding on.

After several minutes, he bowed his head. He asked God to deliver his friend from his suffering. He didn't ask for a miraculous healing or for Jack to live as long as possible. *That would be selfish. More than anything else, I don't want him to suffer. Please, Lord, take away his suffering, however You see fit. You know best. I love You and know You love him at least as much as I do. Thanks for such a great friend. Amen.*

When he looked up, Jack's head was bowed and his eyes shut. He felt for Jack's pulse. "Hey, what are you doing?"

"Just – ah, never mind. What were *you* doing?"

"Praying."

"Yeah? Can't say I blame you."

"Not for *me*, you dodo."

Varrick stiffened, but still held his friend's hand. "Hey, that's *Mister* Dodo to you. Who were you praying for?"

"The Eagles, Coach Rodriguez, a certain teammate."

"Oh yeah? Which teammate?"

"Who do you think? You, you Dodo Head."

"Hey, that's—

"I know, *Mister* Dodo Head." Jack suddenly frowned. "Listen, we don't have much time. I need to tell you something, but you got to promise you'll do what I ask."

Varrick knew it was going to be serious advice and the lump in his throat was back, so there was nothing he could say to stop him. All he could manage was a nod.

"You're my best friend in the whole wide world, Varry, so I can tell you this. But, you've got to promise me you'll think about it and give it a try."

Varrick nodded.

"Okay. You know how you got that great hit in practice that sailed over my head?"

"Uh, yeah."

"That was the *real* you. You hit the ball and ran the bases like you owned them. Whatever you were doing then you have to start doing again. I've heard you talk to yourself out there during practice, especially whenever you're bored. But during games you act like a different person. You look nervous whenever the game is on the line. Be your self. Your old Dodo Head self."

Varrick was working up the strength to give a smart Aleck retort, but he had too much to think about; not just about baseball, but also

83

about his whole approach to life. There was silence for the longest time. Finally, Varrick sort of came back to consciousness.

When he grasped Jack's hand, it felt limp. He felt for a pulse, but there was nothing. Panicking, he looked for a way to call a doctor or nurse. He saw a box with a button on it resting on the end table on the other side. Before leaving Jack's side, he raised his arm up and placed it underneath the sheet. He tucked it in and walked around to the other side and pushed the black button. He stood over his friend and tried remembering his last few words: "Be your self. Your old Dodo Head self." *What a friend! His last minute on earth he spent giving me advice. No complaints or panicking, just advice to his best buddy.*

A nurse strode into the room and headed for Jack. She untucked the sheet and held his wrist for twenty seconds. She turned to Varrick. "Was he your brother?"

Varrick began to shake his head when the word suddenly struck him and its ultimate meaning registered. *Was*, as in no longer *is*. As in *dead*. The shock struck him so hard he had to grip the chair.

Then, holding his head with both hands, he asked over and over and louder and louder, "Why, why, why? Why, George? Why, why, why? Why, George? Why?"

When Marjorie O'Connell and the Bryants entered the room, he was still repeating it. He wouldn't stop until fifteen minutes later when a shot delivered by the attending doctor knocked him out.

Chapter

15

Things actually got worse for me after the hospital incident. Not only did my best friend die at the ripe old age of ten, I had to spend that entire night in the hospital *under observation.*

Miss Bevins, the school psychologist, visited me. She asked a bunch of questions and took lots of notes. No one was allowed in the room while she tested me. They let me leave the hospital after 24 hours, but only after I agreed to see Miss Bevins every day.

On top of all this, I heard some especially bad news the next day when I went over to Larry Jasper's. Mrs. Hicks answered the door and looked at me strangely when I asked if I could see him. "He's not here and I don't expect him back," she whispered through the crack in the door. "He done run away. He on his own now." The door closed and didn't open again, even though I knocked several times.

As if that wasn't enough bad news, the Krupt Brothers saw me and chased me home, threatening and calling me all kinds of names. I felt like a prisoner in my own home. A guy can only take so much. I didn't know what to do about everything, so I went to my room, barricaded my door, and talked to George. I pleaded with him to give me just a few minutes alone with my father. I must've begged for over an hour. First kneeling and then laying on the floor for the longest time, I told him about everything.

Right when I'd given up, when I'd wiped away my tears, and unbarricaded my door, George appeared. Sitting on the couch and wearing his white suit, he looked at me the way Miss Bevins had in the hospital. "Varrick, you've been through quite an ordeal and I want to help. Some things you've asked for I can't help you with, so you are going to need to be patient. I'm limited in what I can do."

I wasn't feeling all that sorry for myself anymore, but I *was* feeling angry because I started yelling: "You're an angel, for crying out loud; an honest-to-goodness angel! Don't tell me you're limited. You can do all kinds of stuff we can't do."

George looked really sad and stared at the carpet awhile, and then motioned for me to join him on the couch, which I did. "I need to explain a few things to you, Varrick. You have several false notions. In some ways, we're *more* limited than you. We can't just fly around and do what we want when we want. We're limited by the instructions we receive."

His words calmed me. I was starting to understand that he wasn't Superman. I cleared my throat and blew my nose. "You can't do whatever you want?"

"We can, but there would be dire consequences."

"Have you ever done something on your own?"

"No."

"What would happen if you did?"

"I'd be banished."

"Banished?"

"From Heaven."

"Why?"

"For not following His plan."

"I heard Satan was an angel once."

"He still *is* an angel. He's a fallen angel; he and those who went with him."

"What did he do wrong?"

"He wanted to run the whole show. You have a saying here on Earth – too big for your britches? Satan got to be too big for his britches, and so God banished him from His presence."

George explained all kinds of things to me. Some of them I understood, some I pretended to understand. I didn't ask many questions because I didn't want him to stop telling me all this "inside information." I remember what he told me about his powers though. "Our main purpose is to deliver messages and protect those people whom

God has chosen to help."

"Why don't you help everyone all the time?"

"God is not a dictator. He gave man free will. If we angels always helped people, you'd all be puppets and no longer have the ability to choose between right and wrong. God loves man so much that He lets him make his own decisions. He hopes he'll make the right ones, but He knows humans aren't always going to. Sometimes He sends us to help humans do right, but they don't always accept help."

I was stunned by all this talk about things I had only imagined. "You mean you visit *other* people, too?"

"There are people I help in the past and other people I help in the future, but right now your father is my one client."

I rose and knelt on the couch beside him. "You see my dad regularly?"

He laughed. "I see him all the time."

I jumped up and reached for George, but there was nothing but air. "How does he look? The same?"

George laughed. "You might say he looks the same. He's just not in his mortal body. Listen, I can't tell you about certain things until... until you're no longer here."

"But he's okay?"

"He's more than okay."

I tried not to tip my hand too much. I sat down and asked casually, "Can I see him for a few minutes sometime?"

Without hesitating, he answered, "No."

I crumbled right then and there, like I had at the hospital. I dropped to the floor and beat it with my fists and begged George through my tears. I was feeling so mad and hopeless that I didn't hear anything. Just flailed away at the hardwood floor with my fists long after they started hurting. I had no idea if George was still around, but I was made aware of my two sisters and two others – my mom and Miss Bevins. I guess Deirdre had been listening at my door again and got my mom to listen, too. Then Mom called Miss Bevins and she got there in a matter of minutes.

After Mom took the girls outside for a talk, Miss Bevins and I also had a talk. She asked me lots of questions. I told her exactly what had happened and what George and I had discussed. The more I told her, the more notes she wrote on her pad. After she filled up about five pages, she excused herself and closed my door. I tip toed over and listened as best I could. She got on the phone and called someone.

◎ ◎ ◎

Cindy Bevins whispered into the phone. "I can't talk now, but I've got a lot to tell you. I really need your help. Call me at home in about fifteen minutes, okay?" She hung up and found Marjorie in the backyard where she was sitting with the girls. Cindy took her aside. "I'm getting Varrick some help, but it'll take time. Call me if he gets hysterical again. You have my home number."

◎ ◎ ◎

Paul Gayle leaned back in his swivel chair and listened intently to Cindy Bevins. He took in her description of Varrick O'Connell – 'a kind, gentle, bright boy who has had a great deal of travail and tragedy the past two and a half years' - without his usual squirming. Cindy's naiveté and way of simplifying complex situations often caused him to lose focus. Today, however, he knew the stakes were too high for that. Here was a boy who could make a perfect case study for the research project he'd been planning for such a long time. He needed a prepubescent boy between nine and twelve who'd experienced a tragedy in his life and had been having delusions - a boy verbal and sensitive enough to tolerate observation and treatment. His mother sounded cooperative.

"She desperately wants help for him," Cindy said. "She told me she's willing to do whatever it takes."

Paul swiveled and stared at his reflection in the large window that gave a spectacular view of Napa Valley. Yet, he didn't notice the acres of greenery spreading out below him. All he saw was his likeness swiveling back and forth thoughtfully. He stopped when a critical point occurred to him. "You *did* broach the subject of shock therapy for Barrick, right?"

"Well, no. Not yet. And it's Varrick, honey; not Barrick, Varrick."

"What the hell kind of name is that, anyway?" He hated to be corrected, especially by Cindy.

"Well, I think it's Irish. Their name is O'Connell."

He repeated it quietly several times as Cindy continued describing the test results and her observations of him at the game, the hospital, and a few minutes earlier at the O'Connells'. He rocked back and forth and uttered the name; a name, he told himself, that would bring him the notoriety and credit he deserved.

Chapter

16

Varrick wrote a letter to his father on the first page of his ninth book of journals:

Dear Dad,

I have so many problems I can hardly count them. First of all, Jack's gone. Then, Larry ran away. The Krupt Brothers hassle me every chance they get. Deirdre's been breaking up my models and anything else of mine she can get her hands on. I have to see the school counselor Miss Bevins every day, and now something else is about to happen. I'm not sure what, but Miss Bevins and Mom have been talking about something for a while now.

I made it through Jack's funeral at St. Joseph's without too much trouble – if you don't call having to run out of a funeral mass to puke not much trouble.

I do have some good news: There's going to be a playoff between the Leviathans and us. I guess the league office wasn't thrilled with the outcome of our last game. The ump hadn't gotten a good look at that last play of me sliding into home, so the league president announced another game would be played in the next week or two. Coach told us to take a couple days off from practice, and then he's going to whip us into shape. He really thinks we'll beat them this time. Dad, I miss you so much! I wish I could just have one hour alone with you, but George won't let me. I love you more than words can express.

Take care,
Varrick

◎ ◎ ◎

Two deputies rang the O'Connell doorbell at nine o'clock one July evening and asked Marge if Varrick was home. "Yes, he is. I'll get him for you. Is he in some kind of trouble?"

Sergeant Wilson, the more outgoing of the two, said they were there to follow a lead in a missing-person case. "We just have a couple questions for your son," he said good-naturedly. He was usually the one who played the good cop. Officer Palermo was the strong, silent type who played "bad cop." He stood stone-faced as Marge went to get Varrick.

After Marge introduced the boy to the officers, she invited them in. They sat on the Early American sofa as Wilson read questions from his steno pad. "When was the last time you saw Larry Jasper?" was first, followed by, "When did you last visit his home?" Varrick described his visit the day before to Larry's when Mrs. Hicks had told him Larry had run away and would never be back.

Palermo asked pointedly, "You *do* know why she said that, don't you?"

"No, sir, I don't."

Wilson smiled. "Larry and Mrs. Hicks did not have an amicable conversation the last time they spoke. Mrs. Hicks is pressing charges."

Varrick waited for them to explain. He'd been taught by his father not to question cops. "If they want you to know something, they'll tell you. If you ask them a question, they might suspect you of something." His words rang in Varrick's ears as he waited for an explanation.

Palermo said bluntly, "We have reason to believe that your friend pulled a knife on Mrs. Hicks."

"Oh my," Marge gasped. She mentally made a note to tell Varrick not to associate with Larry again.

The questioning ended when it became clear Varrick hadn't had contact with Larry for over a week. They thanked Marge and gave her the station phone number in case they encountered Larry or had more information to give.

91

After the officers left, Marge told Varrick he could never see his friend again. "But, Mom, what if he didn't do what they said? What if Mrs. Hicks is lying?"

Marge answered nervously, but emphatically, "You heard what I said: no fraternizing with that boy ever again!"

"Okay, Mom," was all he could say.

⊚ ⊙ ⊚

Late that night, Varrick had a nightmare, awoke with a start and bolted upright. He had been dreaming that all three Krupt Brothers were trying to break into his bedroom. They'd been tapping on the window at the foot of his foldout couch. He avoided looking at the glass for fear he'd see them peering in. As he took a breath to soothe his nerves, a tap on the glass did occur, making him jump. It stopped for a few seconds, but then started up again. Varrick lay down, covering himself with his quilt. The tapping continued, but now there was an accompanying voice. It was a hoarse whisper with a southern accent. Varrick knew only one person who sounded like that - Larry Jasper.

Getting up from the bed, he peered down and saw his friend. Kneeling down to push up the sash, he grunted from the effort. "What in tarnation are you doing here?" he asked. Tarnation was a word he'd learned from Larry.

"Can I come in? It's important. It'll just take a minute." Larry looked desperate.

"Hold on," Varrick whispered. He jumped to his feet and barricaded his door with a chair. Returning to the window, he tried helping his much heavier friend through the opening. After they sat on the pullout mattress, Varrick asked, "Where have you been? The cops are looking for you."

Tired and beleaguered, Larry replied, "That's why I came over. I wanted you to know where I'm staying 'til I figure out what to do." He turned to look at the barricaded door, then the open window. "You know where BBQ's is?"

"Yeah." Everyone in Yuccaville knew about BBQ's, a once-popular outdoor barbecue and beer garden located a hundred yards down

Yuccaville Boulevard from where Varrick's dad had been hit by the drunk driver.

Larry leaned forward. "You know the three little houses in the back? I'm staying in the middle one."

BBQ'S had closed in June at the height of the season. Rumor had it that one of the owners had embezzled thousands of dollars and fled to Mexico.

Images of embezzlers fleeing the U.S. and Larry hiding out in an abandoned house whirled in Varrick's head, making him giddy. His heart raced and his palms began sweating. "You could be arrested for breaking into BBQ's even if you aren't found guilty for threatening Mrs. Hicks with a knife."

"Say what?"

He described what Mrs. Hicks had reportedly told the police. "Isn't that what happened?"

"She turned everything backwards. *She's* the one who pulled the knife. I'm in bigger trouble than I thought."

Varrick started eyeing the chair wedged under the doorknob and wondered if it would hold. Panic arose and his vision blurred. He took a breath, but that only made it worse. "Look, Larry, I'd love to help but…"

Larry looked at him with gratitude and sincerity. "I need your help, but I don't want you in trouble. You stay out of this. I don't want you in danger."

Varrick was prepared to do anything to help his friend, whom he saw as a victim of evil. He wasn't going to stand by while he was convicted of crimes he hadn't done. Varrick imagined Mrs. Hicks' head sprouting devil's horns as he recalled the series of recent conversations he had had with Larry's foster mother through the narrow opening in her front door.

"What do you need?" he asked.

Larry took awhile to answer. "I've been in that one-bedroom house for a whole week and I really need company. You're the only person I trust to not go running to the police. I just need your company and advice."

Varrick knew he meant advice as to how not to be a victim of Mrs. Hicks' lying and wrath. Larry could easily end up in California Youth

Authority until age 18 just for the alleged threat to a foster parent. It would strictly be his word against hers, and it was understood that he'd be the loser should it come to that.

"How are you eating?" Varrick asked.

"Plenty of food was left in the house."

"How did you get in?"

"The back window was left unlocked. I just climbed in after checking that no one was living there. I think the owners used those houses as their bachelor pads. You wouldn't believe some of the stuff I found."

Varrick was glad Larry didn't explain more because he already knew enough to convict his friend of all kinds of things. Varrick told him he'd visit the next day after sunset.

"Perfect. No one will spot you. I better be blasting off. Thanks, ol' friend." It always killed Varrick when he called him that. Without a sound, he slipped out the window and disappeared into the night.

◎ ◉ ◎

The next morning Varrick woke up earlier than usual, sensing something was wrong. It seemed too still to him. He took the chair away from the door and tiptoed to the hall. His mother's whispered voice was amplified because of the linoleum kitchen floor. He slipped into the restroom between the hall and kitchen and sat on the toilet. He could tell the conversation was urgent and about him.

"Yes, I'm concerned, Miss Bevins. Have you spoken to Dr. Gayle about the results of the tests you gave him? What did he think?" There was a long silence. He couldn't stand the tension, so he considered returning to his room, but she started speaking again. "How far away is Napa State Hospital? How long would he have to be under observation?"

Varrick disliked hearing her line of questioning, so he was grateful when she began ending the conversation. "Thanks for everything. He'll be there today for his appointment. We'll talk more later. Good-bye." Varrick's head was spinning with too many thoughts and questions. It was almost too much to bear. He decided to act normal, so he flushed. "Varrick? Is that you?"

He couldn't bear to answer, knowing he'd sound as if he'd been eaves-dropping, so he turned on the sink and thoroughly washed his hands. A knock sounded as he was rinsing them off. Marge never knocked on the bathroom door. She was a very private person and extended privacy to her kids, who didn't take advantage of it much, just when they felt they had to. "Do you want me to make you breakfast before I go to work?"

He felt guilty now, but had no choice but to fib. "No, I'm not hungry, Mom. Thanks."

"Is there anything you need?"

"No, Mom. See you tonight."

"Okay. Don't forget about Miss Bevins."

"I won't." He sat on the tub's edge and counted to five before he heard her walk to her bedroom. A minute later, she walked by again and said good-bye.

Varrick sat on the hard ledge until his bottom became numb. As he stood and waited for the prickly feeling to subside, he reviewed his options. The only one that made any sense was running away. With Larry's muscles and his brains, he figured they could do okay in Mexico. The hardest part would be getting there without being caught.

Chapter 17

Just after eight o'clock, as the sun was setting behind the Tehachapi Mountains, I slid onto my banana seat and coasted down the street on my new Stingray bike, stopping at Boulevard Liquors to buy candy. Since Larry was a fan of anything sweet, I'd have no trouble finding something he liked. Crossing the boulevard, I parked my bike next to the door. Since there wasn't a bike stand and the storeowner wouldn't let me bring my bike in, I had to leave it on the sidewalk.

Boulevard Liquors was more of a market than a liquor store that catered mainly to neighborhood kids. There was always a supply of almost any candy or ice cream a kid would want. I needed only two minutes to spend my two bucks, buying an RC Cola, two Looks, a box of jujubes, two sour apple sticks, two watermelon sticks, two Abba-Zabba bars, a box of Red Vines, a Sidewalk Sundae, and a slew of jawbreakers.

I carried the candy by the tops of the four bags. I knew the owner wouldn't give me a large bag even if I asked. Backing out the door and wondering how I could navigate my bike across the boulevard with my hands full, I stopped dead in my tracks. Pacing first to the east end of the building to peer around the corner, I turned and went to the western corner. I jumped when I saw the last people I wanted to see – the three Krupt Brothers - standing on the dirt beyond the tiny parking lot.

They faced the opposite direction and were examining something. Tony, the youngest, turned and saw me. He nudged Danny and said something. The three boys turned together and it was all I could do to keep from jumping again. Despite my attack of nerves, I managed to see the object of their attention was a bicycle. Which one exactly, I was certain. The three tightened up their ranks, no doubt to hide my brand-new Stingray.

I was paralyzed and speechless. It took all my resolve not to drop my bags. The inevitable finally happened – Bobby yelled: "What are you lookin' at, ya homo?" The other two laughed like hyenas, which was exactly what I would think of them later when I had the chance - smirking, laughing, dangerous hyenas.

The only consolation to their having my bike was that they wouldn't chase me. Not now anyhow. I had two choices: I could approach them and get beaten up for the third time in a week or I could turn tail. It wasn't a hard decision. I took two steps forward and then turned toward the boulevard. More hyena hilarity ensued along with more taunting and clever remarks: "O'Connell, come back here with that candy," "Yeah, we're hungry," "What are you afraid of?"

I crossed the boulevard and thought of Dad. I always thought of him whenever I crossed Yuccaville Boulevard. I usually pictured a drunk losing control of his car and scaling the concrete median to plow into my father.

When I reached the other side, I dared to look back at the three hyenas hovering around their new prey. It was all I could do to keep from crying.

I stepped over the low fence behind BBQ's and managed to not drop anything. Arriving at the three white cabins quicker than I wanted to, I hid behind the eastern cabin and caught my breath. I realized Larry would know something was wrong if I didn't calm down. After counting to one hundred, I took a couple of deep breaths and then approached the front door with the number 2 on it and knocked.

Larry, on the lookout, opened the door immediately. "My man made it. Larry's glad to see you. C'mon in." Larry spoke of himself in the third person when he said something that expressed feelings for someone close to him.

He immediately gave me a tour of the place, which had three rooms more than Larry had told me about the night before. There was a tiny front room with a ladder-back chair and an end table Larry was using as a desk. Behind it was a kitchenette with a gas stove. He showed me the

97

pots and pans stored below. Next to the kitchenette was a bathroom with a sink, toilet, and bathtub. Then, he showed me the bedroom, which had the same beige carpet as the other rooms, but was less threadbare. A double bed with dingy sheets dominated the room and allowed only enough room for another end table. On it was a stack of Playboys.

Larry picked one up and said, "I don't know if you're old enough to look at these yet. I'll let you look at *this* though." He pulled a fountain pen out of his pocket and handed it to me. I looked at the picture of the woman in the bathing suit, but couldn't detect what was special about it. Fountain pens were not yet rare in 1965. "Can't figure out the secret? I'll show you." He turned it upside down, causing the dark ink hiding the woman's body to disappear. She was now naked. As he turned it upright, the navy-blue liquid clothed her curvaceous body again.

"Pretty boss, huh?" Larry looked around at his new digs. I didn't answer because I felt sorry for him. Larry had had no contact with the outside world, no one to share his new pad with. "What do ya think, V-Man?"

Not knowing how else to answer without insulting him, I said, "Pretty boss." Without looking at Larry I asked, "How long are you planning on staying here?"

As he looked around the almost empty bungalow, his smile disappeared. "I figure I can hide out for at least a month. Maybe the rest of the summer."

"Then what?" I hated to rain on his parade, but I didn't know when I'd have another chance to discuss this.

"That's where Larry needs your help. You're good at figuring things out."

I had an idea almost immediately. Not just a way to help Larry, but a way Larry could help me too. "Listen, Lair, we need *each other's* help. I wasn't going to tell you, but my bike was stolen a few minutes ago."

"Yeah? Who? I'll kill him."

I relished the image of Larry beating Bobby and his brothers to a pulp. "That'll only get you in more trouble. I just don't know another way of getting it back."

Larry offered to get it back as soon as it got completely dark. "Don't worry. Larry takes care of the people he loves."

I was touched by the gesture, but I knew time was vital. I could only stay so long and the Krupts couldn't get too big of a jump on Larry. "I better get going. I'll stay longer next time."

"Before you split, tell me where the Corrupts are."

I laughed at Larry's pronunciation. Not knowing whether he said it that way on purpose, I didn't ask, liking to think it was intentional. "They're across the street, next to the liquor store."

He smiled. "Good. I'll pay 'em a visit as soon as you split."

"Then consider me gone. I'm a goner. I'm going, going, gone. Be careful, Lair. Don't get in any more trouble than you're... well, you know what I mean. Take it easy."

"You, too, bro. Larry loves you, Man." He bear-hugged me and then slapped me some skin.

I remembered my bike. "I don't know what I'm gonna tell my mom."

"Don't tell her anything, your bike may show up real soon." His face tightened. "How am I going to get it back to you without your mom or the cops seeing me? Tell you what, come back in an hour and I'll have it for you."

◎ ⊙ ◎

I slipped through a space in the fence where someone had kicked out three slats. Under the cover of darkness I trudged across the patch of desert bridging BBQ's and the Little League field. Taking the long way home, I couldn't block out memories of the several hassles I'd had with the Krupts. I prayed my bike would somehow return safely and that Larry would return unharmed, too.

Twenty minutes later, I rounded the final bend and tramped up my driveway. A hissing sound came from the area where the Krupts had pounced on me a few days ago. It was a whisper that called out my name. As I followed the sound, I bumped into and fell over something hard and metal. It was my bike! At the end of the alley I could barely make out the retreating form of a man hissing over his shoulder. "Piece-a-cake, Varrick. Larry loves you, man."

I stared at the corner of the house Larry had just disappeared around and felt a warm glow. It was the sensation I felt whenever someone sacrificed something for me, or God answered a prayer. I then realized this was probably a case of both.

Chapter

18

Varrick had no sooner parked his bike alongside the family car and locked the garage when a bright light shone in his face. Trying to keep from cringing while holding up a hand to shield his eyes, he heard a voice. "Are you Barrack O'Connell?" It was a policeman. The voice sounded so gruff and mean that all he could think to say was "Yes."

As the light shut off and two doors slammed, Varrick stood frozen in front of the garage. It was only after the mispronouncing policeman asked, "Can we step inside where it's light?" that he shook off the shock. When the boy and two men reached the porch, the front door opened to reveal Marge's face full of worry. "What is going on?"

The husky cop answered, "Good evening, ma'am. We had a report of a runaway boy seen in the vicinity and we've come to check it out."

"Runaway boy? Do you know anything about this, Varrick? Is this your Negro friend they're asking about?"

Before he could clear his throat to answer, Marge turned to the cops. "What's the boy's name, officer?"

Flipping open his writing pad, the cop read, "Larry Jasper, age 13. Five-feet, nine inches, 160 pounds, medium-dark Negro with short, nappy hair."

Marjorie folded and unfolded her hands. She looked at her son expectantly. "Well? Did you see him just now?"

Varrick contemplated how he could dodge her question without lying. "I saw someone in the dark before the policemen got here, but I didn't get a good look."

The husky voiced officer bent over Varrick. "Barrack, you're a good friend of Larry Jasper's, correct?"

"Yes, sir."

"And you don't honestly know if it was him you saw?"

"Well, I can't say for sure. It's almost pitch-black."

"Young man," he began, "we are very busy and do not have time to play 'Twenty Questions,' understand?"

"Yes."

"Yes, what?"

"Yes, Sir."

"That's better. Now, either you tell us the whole truth and nothing but the truth, or we take you to the station for questioning. Is that clear?"

Varrick tried saying the word 'yes' when Marge spoke. Her voice lost its softness and now had an edge; an edge Varrick knew only too well. He thought she was about to yell at him, so he took a step away from her. At the end of her first sentence he relaxed. "Now wait just a minute, officers. You can't bully my son. I know our rights. If the boy says he isn't sure whether or not he saw his friend, then we take his word for it. We are not going to answer any more of your questions without an attorney present."

All three males stared at Marge in disbelief. The quiet cop elbowed the talkative one and motioned for them to leave. He quietly followed, and it was only when they reached the curb that he exclaimed, "Hell hath no fury like a mother scorned."

Varrick had never seen his mother tell anyone off and he wanted to savor the moment. However, it was cut short when she tugged him by the shirtsleeve. "Let's go inside. You have a lot of explaining to do."

◎ ⊙ ◎

Varrick rocked on his knees so long that they became numb; impervious to the pain he had subjected them to for the past hour and a half. Alternately sobbing and praying, he was at the end of his rope. Being grounded for not telling his mother the truth about Larry's whereabouts was not what troubled him. The pathos of his existence – the tragic turn his life had taken – anguished him. Not only had his father died senselessly at the hands of a drunk, his best friend – Jack Bryant – had also died. His second-best friend – Larry Jasper – ran away from home and was being hunted by the police. On top of all that, the Krupts had stolen his new bike and were likely to do it again.

His tears were not the products of the temporary defeat a boy indulges in when he thinks no one is watching. Nor were they the fruits of self-pity when he realizes how bad his life has become. Varrick O'Connell's outburst was an involuntary paroxysm comprised of equal parts terror, rage, pain, and defeat. These feelings had been buried for the two and a half years since his father had died, and were pouring out of every cell of his being.

The object of his fury was God. "Why, Lord? Why do all these things happen to me? What did I do to deserve any of it? Why do You hate me so much that You're having me suffer like this?" The words spilled out furiously and continued for several minutes as Varrick rocked back and forth on the thin carpet covering the hardwood floor. He didn't think to muffle his cries, but pressed the heels of both hands on his temples as he rocked furiously. Leaning forward so far that his head touched his knees, he covered both eyes and cried. He gulped for air since his nose was full of mucus.

His sobs were so loud he couldn't hear the two other sounds in his room – the television and a man's voice. The TV voice was announcing a show was about to begin, but the voice of the man in the room spoke in a whisper that conveyed concern and love. He repeated a simple sentence ten times before Varrick actually realized his presence: "It's all right, Son."

When the voice entered his consciousness, Varrick's sobbing dropped in volume. He uncovered his eyes and straightened. His arms dropped to his sides and he stared in disbelief at the man who knelt before him.

"It's going to be all right, Varrick. *Everything* is going to be all right, Son. Trust me."

Varrick could neither believe nor accept that three feet away knelt the person he had loved most in his life - his greatest hero, his inspiration, the man responsible for his life – his father.

"Dad?"

"Yes, Son."

"It's you?"

Chuckling slightly, he said, "It's me."

Varrick replied, "It's you. It's *really* you... But...I don't understand...I thought..."

"Thought I was dead? Gone forever?"

The boy nodded.

"Well, I'm no longer dead, but I'm not alive like you and Mom and the girls. I'm alive in another realm."

"So...you *are* here? I'm not imagining this?"

"I'm here."

Varrick stared at the familiar image of his father. He didn't look a single iota different from all of the times he'd seen him alive. He fought back the urge to hug his father's form because he didn't want to do anything to jinx the situation, to violate the unknown rules that might somehow govern their meeting.

"How'd you get here, Dad?"

His facial expression shifted from a bemused smile to a blank stare. After a long pause he shrugged and said, "I have no idea."

"Do you know how long you're going to be here?"

Padraig O'Connell shrugged his narrow shoulders. "As far as I can tell, we don't have time there. By the way, how long ago *did* I die?"

"Two years, eleven months, and two days."

"It seems like just yesterday I was crossing the Boulevard when everything went black. And yet it also seems like I've always been in the bosom of Abraham."

Varrick came down off of his knees and sat straight-legged. "The what of who?"

"The bosom of Abraham. That's what it's called."

Varrick made a move to kneel again out of excitement, but his aching knees reminded him of the impossibility of reassuming that posture. He resumed sitting. "Are you in heaven or..."

No, I'm not in Hell. I'm in the Lord's presence, Son. And when final judgment comes, I'll be in Heaven forever."

As compelling as the topic was, Varrick thought of a more pressing one. "Dad, do you have a guardian angel?"

"Yes. In fact, I understand you met George already."

"Twice. He told me there was no way you could come see me. He said it had never before been allowed by You-Know-Who."

"What he told you is right. That's why I can't figure out why I'm here." He remained sitting and took in the entire room with a 360-degree turn of his head. Varrick wanted to ask his dad how he did that, but he didn't want to waste any of their precious time together. "Gee, Varrick, this room hasn't changed at all." His eyes fixed on the wall of pictures and plaques. "Do you sleep here?"

Varrick pointed to the pullout couch.

"I forgot that thing pulls out. We rarely ever used it. I wonder why your mother didn't redecorate."

"I like it the way it is. Besides, she hardly ever comes in here."

"How is she, Son?"

"She's fine. You want to see her?"

"Of course I do, but I can't. You're the only one who can see and hear me."

"Wow. How come?"

"I'm not sure exactly." Furrowing his brow, he asked, "Are you having some kind of trouble?"

Varrick lowered his gaze. "It just seems like the most important people in my life keep leaving. And there are these three brothers who keep bothering me, but you don't want to hear about that."

"So that's why I'm here. I guess there *are* things I can do better than George. Tell me what's going on."

Without hesitation Varrick launched into describing his life since the summer of 1962. After he finished, Padraig sighed and began to speak. "That's more than anyone should have to go through, much less a ten-year-old boy."

"Eleven," Varrick interjected.

"Before I know it you'll be in high school. Then college, then…" His face went slack, realizing he wouldn't be sharing his son's future. He then girded himself for what he was about to say. "Son, I was allowed to come here today instead of George because there are lessons that angels can't teach because they never learned them in the first place."

"What kinds of lessons, Dad?"

"Lessons only a father can teach, Varrick."

His eyes lit up with the realization that he was finally going to receive help. His father began by explaining that Varrick's problems were not simple and that since they had piled up over a long period of time they weren't going to miraculously and suddenly disappear. "But, they *will* get better and you *will* learn to cope with certain situations and certain people better. What did you say those boys' names were? I'll show you how to deal with them."

Varrick and his father stood as the spirit of Padraig O'Connell began demonstrating techniques that he had learned from his father when he was a boy; techniques that would change - for better or worse - how Varrick O'Connell would deal with the curveballs he'd have to face both on the ball field and in the other arenas of his life. It was a time that Varrick would remember and cherish for the rest of his many years on Earth.

Chapter

19

Marjorie O'Connell fingered the tape reel resting on the seat beside her as she drove to her appointment with Cindy Bevins. She was nervous for two reasons: because she'd broken her promise not to hear the recording before Miss Bevins could, and that listening to it revealed how disturbed Varrick had become. She realized his obsession with his father's death had worsened to the point where he was having imaginary discussions that included sobbing and giddy laughter. She knew how the psychologist would interpret it, but she wasn't sure which measures to take.

They had talked about various interventions, including hospitalization, but Marge had dismissed those as worst-case solutions that would probably never happen. But now that she had proof of her son's emotional and psychological imbalance she knew that what she once considered a remote possibility was now more than likely to happen. She momentarily considered tossing the tape reel out the window and returning to work as if the breakdown hadn't ever occurred.

However, she wasn't the only one besides Cindy Bevins who knew of the tape and her son's irrational behavior. Deirdre had witnessed his sobbing and conversing with the imagined ghost of his deceased father. She'd reported the incident to the psychologist without telling her mother, who hadn't any clue of the episode until Miss Bevins called her the night before.

◎ ◎ ◎

Cindy Bevins pushed 'Stop' on her recorder after listening to Varrick plead, "Why, Lord? Why do all these things have to happen to me?

What did I do to deserve any of this? Why do You hate me so much that You're making me suffer?" She then pushed the fast-forward button until the counter reached '1090.' Punching 'Play,' she heard: "It's you. It's *really* you... But... I don't understand... I thought..." followed by a long silence interrupted by: "So... you *are* here? I'm not imagining all this?" After another pause, she heard the boy ask, "How'd you get here, Dad?"

Continuing to listen to the tape, the psychologist wrote detailed notes, sometimes rewinding the tape before replaying a segment again.

Although the clock in her office read "10:30 PM," she continued scribbling notes and pushing buttons. After reviewing the tape a second time, Cindy called Paul Gayle. They spoke for over an hour, hanging up around twelve-thirty.

◉ ⊙ ◎

Varrick bounded into the living room with good news. "Guess what, Mom? We get to play a final game against the Leviathans. Admission will be charged and all proceeds will go to kids who have the same disease as Jack had. It's being called 'The Jack Bryant Memorial League Championship Game.' What do you think?"

Marjorie smiled weakly. "Varrick, we need to talk. Sit down, Honey."

As excited as he was about a last chance to redeem himself against the Leviathans, Varrick knew better than to change the subject back to baseball. He could tell by his mother's demeanor that she would not be deterred from her mission to tell him something she considered important.

She explained that a psychologist recommended by Cindy Bevins would examine him. "He's supposed to be very good. He's been in Newsweek Magazine and specializes in kids."

Looking at his mother in disbelief, Varrick stammered. "Y-Y-You're going to have me put in a loony bin?"

"Honey, you'll just stay there long enough to be tested and diagnosed. I don't know what else to do. Miss Bevins says it's the only option." Her face brightened as she changed the subject. "Now, what's this about a special ball game?"

Varrick's face was a counterpoint to his mother's. "I won't be able to play now. Our big chance to finally beat Big R is ruined."

Marjorie reached over and stroked her son's close-cropped hair and whispered, "Honey, don't make this any harder than it already is." Fighting back the urge to acquiesce without any explanation, Varrick sat up and said, "Mom, I know you're doing what you think is best, but I really *did* talk to Dad. He sat right next to me on the floor in my bedroom and said he was in the bosom of Abraham, wherever that is. He asked about you and the girls and seemed worried about us."

Fighting back tears, Marjorie smiled and hugged her son. "You better get packed for your trip, Honey. We're leaving in the morning."

This time Varrick followed his compliant nature and followed his mother's wishes, even though he wasn't finished trying to convince her he truly *had* spoken to his father. He figured it would only make matters worse to press the issue just now, so he returned her hug and headed for his room.

◉ ☉ ◎

Larry Jasper lay on his side and stared at the wall of his hideaway. Tears streaked his face as he considered his situation: He'd been hiding over a week and it hadn't been the adventure he had hoped for. There was nothing to do, no one to talk to. He might as well be in jail where at least he'd have three meals a day and someone to converse with. "Lord, help me out of this situation. Protect me from Mrs. Hicks' lies. I don't deserve jail and I sure don't deserve to starve to death. Please send help, Father. In Jesus' precious name I pray."

After an hour of wall-watching Larry fell asleep. He dreamed of being in jail, the cell looking just like the room he was sleeping in. Guards were stationed at the door and bars were on the windows. He dreamed of lying on his back and staring at the ceiling while he counted the holes in the acoustic ceiling. When he was well into the hundreds, he heard a tapping sound that caused him to lose count. Giving up his mission, he looked over at the nearest window, which had lost its iron bars. On the other side of the glass beckoning him was Varrick O'Connell. "Pssst. Larry! Let me in before the coyotes get me."

Larry lay chuckling at the thought of his best friend being afraid of coyotes in downtown Yuccaville. Then, he laughed at the absurdity of his dream. "Larry sure has some trippy dreams." He looked over at the window to his right and sat up fast. "You really *are* here!" Jumping out of bed, he pinched himself to make sure he was awake before unlocking the window.

As Varrick crawled through the opening, Larry grabbed his much smaller friend and hugged him. "Larry is so glad to see his little buddy. What's up?"

Varrick answered, "If I don't get some help fast, I'll end up in the booby hatch."

"Well, what can Larry do, Vee?"

"I don't know if you can do *anything*, but I'm afraid if something *isn't* done, I'll end up in Newsweek."

Larry let down his friend. "Say what?"

"I'll explain."

Larry said, "Do me a favor. Start at the beginning."

"Okay. Remember I told you about Miss Bevins?"

"Yeah. You said she's really nice."

"I was wrong. She and her boyfriend have plans for me that include living in a nuthouse."

"What? That don't sound right. What can Larry do?"

Varrick described what had happened since Larry had brought his bike back. The boys discussed their respective dilemmas for over an hour before Varrick slipped out and returned home.

◎ ⊙ ◎

Paul Gayle sat perfectly upright as he typed the outline of a paper he planned to present to the APA. "It'll be my crowning achievement," he thought as he put the finishing touches on the framework. "I'll finally get the recognition I deserve. No more being dismissed as some sort of quack. This will be my big breakthrough."

After grinning gleefully at the thought of his future notoriety, he suddenly grimaced as a thought struck him. "What am I going to call this thing? I need to capture the scientific nature of the subject without sounding overly clinical. The title must have a poetic zing that'll perk up everyone's ears at the convention in September."

"How about 'A Young Boy's World of Delusionary Dementia'? No... too dreary and alliterative. Maybe I could use the kid's name: Varrick, Varrick's... Varrick's Disorder. No, 'disorder' is used too much already. I need a term that's more artistic than scientific."

He pulled his thesaurus from his bookshelf.

Almost settling begrudgingly on the word derangement, he decided it sounded too far-gone. "No, it has to have a serious, but not irrevocable sound; a condition not impossible to cure."

He searched the paperback for several minutes before the word popped out at him. "Disturbance. Not too ominous, not too inconsequential. It rolls off the tongue. 'Varrick's Disturbances.' Perfect."

Gayle slipped a blank sheet of paper into his Royal and stroked the keys. After satisfying himself on the third try, he rolled the title page out of the gray machine and looked at it proudly. "Varrick's Disturbances." He repeated the title twice, adding 'presented by Doctor Paul Gayle, internationally known psychologist and eminent expert of prepubescent delusional disorders.'"

20

I had some things I needed to do before Mom and I would leave for Napa, so I rose at sunrise and slipped out my window. Getting my bike from where I hid it in the alley, I began the two-mile jaunt to the cemetery to visit Jack. As I passed Joshua School, I spotted someone jumping over the fence on the far side. Was it Larry?

Racing to catch up, I pedaled as fast as I could. But by the time I reached the school, he was nowhere to be seen; not on the sidewalk, not at the high school next door, not in the desert across from the school. After searching the outside of both schools, I headed for the cemetery.

When I reached the Catholic section, I was so exhausted that I fell to my knees at Jack's grave. "Hi, ol' buddy, it's me." I looked around to make sure no one was around. "We're getting another chance to play the Leviathans, but guess what? I won't be there. Mom and Miss Bevins think I'm crazy so they're sending me to a nuthouse for extensive testing. With you and Dad gone, no one's on my side, unless you count Larry, and right now no one knows where he's at. Well, enough of my problems. How's everything up there?"

Naturally, I didn't hear a response, but I tried picturing Jack. I was barely able to, so I didn't try imagining what his answer might have been. I sat cross-legged on the grass and attempted picturing my future, but all I could visualize was being hooked up to a huge machine and being zapped and tested, zapped and tested, over and over. I would live in a concrete cell with bars and lose all contact with the outside world. Only Dr. Gayle would be allowed to talk to me, and bread and water would be passed under my cell door. I'd grow old and die there. When people would eventually hear of my passing, they'd say, "He could've been so much more. It's a pity he saw angels and ghosts."

I checked my watch, saw it was already eight o'clock, and stood. Crossing myself, I said a prayer for Jack and told him, "Jackie ol' boy, do me a favor. Put in a good word, alright? You can tell 'em I'm a dodo head, but a *good* dodo head, okay? See ya later, Alligator."

◎ ⊙ ◎

Twenty minutes later, I raced by Joshua School and saw a dark figure emerging from the bushes near the front fence. I knew it could only be one person, so I sped up and headed straight for him. He must've seen me because he jumped back into the bush. About five feet from the hedge, I jumped off my bike and yelled, "Larry, it's Varry. Come out, come out, wherever you are."

I expected him to leap out and scare me, so I watched for him out of the corner of my eye. I patrolled the line of thick bushes, saying, "I know you're in there," and "Ollie, Ollie, oxen, free," waiting for him to spring out.

As well as I kept up my guard expecting him to pounce, I wasn't prepared for my legs being knocked out from under me. Blue sky whizzed by before my head hit the ground so hard I almost passed out. I looked up and saw three forms above laughing at me. I couldn't raise a hand to shield my eyes from the glare.

How could Larry - my best friend now that Jack is gone - lay me out and then laugh hysterically at me? Since my vision was still blurred I saw not one, but three Larrys standing over me and laughing like hyenas - hysterical, sarcastic hyenas.

Wait a minute! I am surrounded by hyenas - three of them. Even though my eyes were still unfocused, I didn't need them to understand the situation. I had been ambushed by the evil Krupt Brothers. Their cackling voices swirled above me. I could pick out phrases such as "panty waist," "chicken s—t," "big baby," and "sissy boy."

I wanted to get as far from them as possible; to jump on my bike and race like the wind away from their twisted, ugly faces and their stupid, hateful comments. But I knew that wasn't going to happen. For

112

one thing, my equilibrium was as bad as a wino's drunk on muscatel. Second, I had no chance of escaping them even if I had been unfazed by the blow to my head. All I could do was lay there until my head unclouded or I passed out. I prayed that if the latter happened the Lord wouldn't let the Krupts beat me too badly.

What happened next was very confusing. The scene shifted drastically; and I mean *drastically*! I suddenly saw two very familiar people – my father and Jack Bryant. The two of them and I were neither in a room nor outdoors. We were floating in a space with a totally different atmosphere and we were suspended in brilliant light. Jack and Dad never looked better. Their faces shone like quartz. They exuded auras that were simultaneously comforting and electrifying. They brimmed with a compassion I'd never witnessed anyone display before.

Jack spoke first. "Hey you. I'd ask you how you are, but I can see the deep doo you're in, Dodo head. But don't worry. It will all work out."

Dad spoke. "That's right, son. Everything *will* work out. You will stand up to these bullies like I showed you. Stand firm. Know that 'He who is in you is greater than he who is in the world.' Remember that, and everything will be okay. We love you, Son."

I couldn't move my lips, so I simply listened. Jack smiled with incredible love. "Your dad speaks the truth. And you know how I know that? Because, he speaks God's truth. When you face the Krupt Brothers in a minute and when you bat against Big R again, remember two things: 'Trust in the Lord with all your heart and lean not on your own understanding,' and 'Even though you pass through the valley of the shadow of death, you will fear no evil'." Their love and kindness enveloped me completely. It was as though I were in a protective, loving soft shell.

Next thing I knew the scene had shifted again back to Yuccaville. I was somehow standing upright, bathed in the bright sunlight on the front lawn of Joshua School, facing my three enemies, who stared at me with curiosity and distrust. If I didn't know better I'd say they were scared. I stood and waited for them to act. They seemed to do the same. I finally asked, "Where's my bike?"

Bobby finally answered. "It's in the bushes."

"I want it back."

He slowly, almost unsurely walked up to me. He then raised his right

113

hand deliberately and poked me in the chest. "Who do you think you are to say you want it back?" He smiled his sarcastic smirk and glanced at his brothers.

All I could do was repeat, "I want it back." Only, this time I added the word "now" for emphasis.

Bobby's eyes widened and he looked impressed. But, the sneer returned. "And if you don't get it back?"

Normally, I wouldn't have had an answer. I might have swallowed hard and shrugged, or swallowed and looked at the ground, or swallowed and smiled while my eyes filled with tears. But I felt differently now. Call it hope, calm, poise, or even insanity. All I know is that the words of my father and Jack reverberated in my mind: "Trust in the Lord with all your heart... He who is in you is greater than he who is in the world." No, check that - the Word of God reverberated in my mind's ear and everywhere inside me.

I began to speak. As I did, I noticed I didn't have the need to swallow. I simply moved my mouth and words came out. It was as if someone were speaking for me: "Bobby, I want my bike back. *Now*. I'm in a hurry."

As Bobby answered, he looked away twice while saying, "And I want to know what you'll do if we don't give it back."

I studied Bobby's face. For the second time since I met him, I felt pity for him. I felt the same as I had when he'd misspelled 'spelling' during the bee. So even though I felt sorry for him and even though I felt fearless, I knew the folly of telling him of my pity for him. He only seemed interested in what I'd do if I didn't get my bike back.

The words came effortlessly. "If I don't have my bike back by the time I count to five, I'll make you wish you'd never taken it in the first place."

Bobby smirked, but more at his brothers than at me. He looked down so as to gather up the strength to do what he did next, which was to shove me. He telegraphed his move so much that I was able to step aside and he fell flat on his face. All I could think of to do was jump on his back. He must've read my mind because he turned onto his back before I could apply all my weight. He struck me with the bottom of his hand just below my right eye, snapping my head back. I felt the tissue instantly beginning to swell. I bore down on him even though he flailed at my chest and head. I grabbed both wrists and pinned them to the lawn.

At that moment I was equal to Bobby Krupt, no longer feeling like a tiny bug about to be smashed by a giant. I actually felt I could handle him. The realization took away from my concentration because I didn't see the left jab land precisely where his earlier blow had connected. All I know is that I fell backward and Bobby pinned me again.

I struggled to get out from under him, but realized the futility. I would have to punch him in the face the way he had done to me. I led with an open hand that caught him on the cheek and succeeded in angering him. He puffed out both cheeks and said, "You've had it now, O'Connell."

Instead of letting his words intimidate me, I literally laughed in his face. I laughed in Bobby Krupt's face! And then I retorted: "*You're the one who's had it.*" I reared back with all my might and socked him between the eyebrows. I knew it hurt because he yelled "Ow" and fell backward. It was now my chance to turn the tables. But instead of jumping on top of him, I decided we would box. I stood over Bobby and said, "Come on, big man. Get up. I'll show you who's going to get it."

If Bobby Krupt's looks could kill, I'd be dead because he gave me the meanest, scariest stare I'd ever seen. But the Lord's words resounded in my head so convincingly that my fear fell away: "He who is in you is greater than he who is in the world."

Bobby slowly got to his feet and approached as if he was about to teach me a lesson in fighting. The only flaw in his plan was the right-left combination I hit him with: the unexpected right jab of a lefty followed by a haymaker that landed him flat on his back.

I stood over him with both fists doubled and my feet far apart. I imagine I looked like a little like Cassius Clay when he had stood over Sonny Liston during their title matches.

Bobby held up his left palm, flinched, and said, "You can have your bike. Just leave me alone."

Instead of ridiculing Bobby with his words, I strode around him and headed for his brothers. Looking them both in the eye, I demanded my bike. What happened next still makes me laugh whenever I remember it: They *both* ran into the bushes and brought my Stingray to me. I half

115

expected them to ask me if I wanted them to wash it. They stared as I climbed onto my banana seat and began to pedal across the thick green grass of Joshua School's front lawn.

I rode like the wind back to my house. Exhilaration started down at my pedaling feet and shot all the way up to my shoulders. For the first time in years, I felt free. Free of fear, free of terror, free of the Krupt Brothers.

Somehow I felt I could face the journey that lay ahead.

Chapter

21

When I slipped back through my bedroom window, it was nine o'clock. My door was still shut. I heard Mom calling to me: "Wake up, Varrick. After you pack, we'll have breakfast."

Feigning drowsiness, I answered, "Okay, Mom." I didn't know exactly what to pack, but I threw some t-shirts, underwear, and Bermuda shorts into my duffle bag with a picture of Dad that I took off my wall. I included a baseball my team signed right before Jack had gotten really sick. It was my most prized possession, even more valuable than my glove.

My mom had fixed breakfast. "Where are the girls?" I asked as I sopped up egg yokes with my toast.

She glanced out the window. "They're around." She sounded tired and distant, her mind somewhere else. Somewhere far away, like maybe Napa State Hospital.

A little later, we stepped off our porch as my sisters appeared. They acted as though Mom and I were merely going for a walk. "Girls," Mom said as we stood by the car, "kiss your brother good-bye." Deirdre looked doubtful, but Mom must've shot her a look because she lurched at me and pecked me on the cheek. Tess stood on her toes and said, "Bye, bye, Varrick."

When I hugged her she made a funny noise. I probably squeezed her too hard, but she just looked down. Deirdre stood far off, acting like something was on her mind. After we pulled out of the driveway, I saw them wave at me through the side mirror. They looked sort of pitiful waving slowly and standing by our big elm. I figured it would be the last I'd see them for a long, long time.

◎ ◎ ◎

As we left town, I said silent good-byes to the Joshua trees that stood in great clumps on both sides of Sierra Highway. I could tell Mom had a lot on her mind. She gripped the wheel tightly and must've been gritting her teeth because her jawbone kept clenching. I'd never seen her look this worried, which is saying something because my mother was a world-class worrier. In an attempt to distract her, I tried small talk. "Where are we meeting this psychologist?"

This didn't seem to be a good topic to take her mind off worrying because she hunched over the wheel even more and flexed her jaw again. Between clenches she replied, "Denny's in Fresno." She took her eyes off the road for a moment and forced a smile. "Honey, why don't you just sit back and take a nap? I'll wake you when we get there."

With nothing else to do besides stare into the desert glare, I said "Okay" and shut my eyes. Pretending to nap, I replayed the good times Jack and I had had together. We'd been as close as brothers, and part of the reason we had been so close was because we didn't have brothers. Sometimes, I reasoned, "blood brothers" like us are even thicker than real ones.

Somewhere around Bakersfield I did fall asleep. I dreamed I was playing the Leviathans again. Instead of being joined by my teammates, however, I played them alone. I played all positions, which of course is impossible, even in dreams. What really made the dream scary was that Ross Ramsey was taller and scarier than in real life. And making matters worse, the first baseman was Tony Krupt, the second baseman Danny Krupt, and the catcher Bobby Krupt. They were all very evil looking and had fangs like wolves. They cackled and slobbered profusely.

The dream went on forever. The scoreboard read "Leviathans 169, Eagles 0" and it was still the first inning! Having to play all nine positions, I was constantly running – from the mound to first to the outfield and back to the infield. My legs were about to collapse. My left leg was a bloody stump. When I asked for a timeout so I could get some first-aid, Coach Rodriguez emerged from the dugout, clucking his tongue, "Eet's too late, amigo. You're going to lose your leg. And your mother's going to kill us both." I was sobbing and sweating profusely and having trouble staying upright.

"Varrick, Varrick! Wake up, honey. We're in Fresno."

I tried opening my eyes, but the glare was so intense that I shut them again. I seemed stuck between two worlds – the nightmarish existence of playing the Leviathans (plus the Brothers Krupt) on one leg and the all-too-realistic Fresno at high noon in the middle of summer with no idea of when or even if I'd return home.

"Honey, what's wrong?"

"Nothing."

She unhooked her seat belt and looked at me with anguish and alarm. "Your clothes are soaked and you're as white as a ghost." After she uttered the word 'ghost,' she flinched self-consciously as if she had offended me.

Surveying the parking lot of gleaming cars, she sighed and said, "Let's go inside. I don't see them out here."

I was puzzled. "*Them?* What do you mean by 'them,' Mom?"

Looking around again, probably so as to not have to face me, she explained, "Doctor Gayle and Miss Bevins."

"Why Miss Bevins? Is she going to ride with Dr. Gayle and me?"

"Yes, she took the Greyhound up here and Dr. Gayle's supposed to pick her up. She'll be staying somewhere near the hospital."

"But why?"

"She wants to spend her vacation with her fiancé."

"Oh," was all I could manage.

Little did I know that Miss Bevins' fiancé was the man who would be studying me.

⊚ ⊙ ⊚

By the time Cindy Bevins arrived at the Fresno bus depot, she had recouped her usual calm. She had been angry when Paul had called her at 4:30 AM to tell her he would not be coming to Yuccaville to pick me up. He hadn't bothered to give an excuse why he had changed his plans – their plans – without asking her opinion. And just like that, she had been reduced to calling Greyhound to book a two-hundred-and-

119

fifty-mile trip to Fresno, where they would meet Marge and Varrick O'Connell.

What pushed the usually calm and demure psychologist over the edge was Paul's insistence that Cindy not catch a ride with the O'Connells. He didn't want the three of them becoming well acquainted. After all, he contended, she couldn't become too familiar with their client. The whole thing didn't make any sense to her. She'd been momentarily tempted to defy his wishes, but he had quenched that possibility when he warned, "Don't even think about calling those people and bumming a ride. You have to keep your professional distance, Sweetie Pie. Don't become attached to those people, especially the boy."

Cindy couldn't begin to count all the things that Paul Gayle had said that had angered her. His arrogance, more than anything else, had inflamed her to the core. He had attained a doctorate in psychiatry, been published in the most prominent journals in the world, and yet had the gall to order her to take a four-hour bus ride on the pretense of keeping a professional image with a boy and his mother!

She had, of course, obeyed him, just as she always had. After all, she told herself, she had too much to lose if she didn't. She owed him virtually everything: her affection and admiration, her professional standing, her job, her college loans, her self-worth. So, it was difficult for her to call Greyhound, but it wasn't the first difficult thing she had to do to maintain peace between her and Dr. Gayle.

Marjorie marched up to the entrance of Denny's as though late for an appointment. She held the door ten seconds for Varrick before he stepped over the threshold in a semi-trance. She wasn't perturbed by his slowness; in fact, she was surprised he hadn't taken longer to complete the trek from the parking lot, given the residual sleepiness from his nap, his recent general disorientation, and the confusion of their situation.

She sympathized with his predicament. He was a good boy who hadn't survived his father's death well. What he needed most was what he had lost – a father. She knew things had been tough for him at school and around the neighborhood, even at home, but she hadn't truly known what his life had been like. No one had, especially Cindy Bevins who had just lately entered his life.

Scouring the dining room of the coffee shop, Marge didn't see the couple. She informed the hostess they'd need a table for four and were expecting two members of their party to arrive shortly.

◎ ⊙ ◎

As she stepped off the bus, Cindy was hit by a blast of heat that nearly drove her back to the air-conditioned comfort of the Greyhound behind her. The second thing striking her was Paul's absence. He had promised to meet her at 11:30. Here it was 12:05 (her bus had arrived late) and he still wasn't anywhere in sight.

She followed the porters inside the depot and sat on her largest trunk. Cindy had packed the metal locker and her two medium-sized suitcases because she was half-expecting to stay in Napa after August. Paul had hinted that they should move up their wedding date to this month, perhaps eloping to Reno.

"What about Varrick?" she had wondered.

"What about him?" he had retorted. "No ten-year-old brat named after military housing will dictate our lives." She hadn't the energy to correct him on all three counts: his age, the fact he isn't a brat, and his name. Paul would have just dismissed her with the wave of his hand anyway.

Another half hour later, Cindy felt a tap on her shoulder. "Let's go, Missy. We got people to see, things to do, places to go. I'll take the trunk, you get the bags."

◎ ⊙ ◎

Marge peered into her coffee cup and debated whether she should ask for a second refill. She glanced at her watch again and caught herself clucking her tongue. Varrick looked up at her expectantly and fought back the temptation to ask her what could be keeping them. It was five minutes before one o'clock and no sign of either.

"I'll be right back, Honey," Marge promised as she stood and headed

121

toward the ladies' room.

Varrick tilted his plastic cup back and caught a clump of ice with his tongue. He was chomping on it when a man's voice above him warned, "You'll ruin your teeth, young man. Believe me, it's not worth it. I know." He turned slowly to see who was giving him the unsolicited advice. It was a short man with a large, round head and brown hair combed straight forward. His cheeks were pock marked from a nasty siege of adolescent acne. His plaid shirt was wrinkled and hung over a pair of khaki chinos that had long ago lost their crease. A pair of Mexican huarache sandals finished off his ensemble.

Varrick's inventory of the stranger didn't last more than a second, but he had already decided he couldn't trust him. His appraisal wasn't based on the man's appearance, but the tone of his voice and his insincere facial expressions. What grabbed Varrick's attention next was a well-manicured hand appearing on the stranger's right shoulder. It belonged to Miss Bevins, who said with forced perkiness, "Hi, Varrick. How are you? Where's your mom?"

Answering her first question by shrugging, he pointed behind him to indicate where his mother most likely might be.

"Good. May we join you?"

◎ ◉ ◎

He fought back the urge to shrug again, but pointed to the other chairs. "Sure."

After both sat down, there was a silence so profound that the air around them seemed to stagnate. The illusion disappeared when Cindy spied Marge returning from the ladies' room. "Oh good, here she comes."

Varrick's stomach churned as he figured the awkward silence between the three of them was a harbinger of things to come. He steadied his hand enough to grip his glass and tilted back his head for a long drink, but wasn't prepared for the speed of the avalanche that hit him teeth-first. Two ice cubes missed its target and tumbled out of the cup, landing on the carpet. "Smooth move, Ex-Lax," the pock marked man intoned.

A half-beat behind was Marge's protest. "Oh, Varrick. Look what you've done." Before she could finish her next sentence – "Pick up the ice, please." – her son had bailed from his seat and tracked down the errant cubes, one under the center of the table and the other directly under Cindy Bevins' chair, to his immediate right. He could sense her above him, angling her body to check his progress. It was more of a symbolic show of support than an actual attempt to steer him to the right place, but Varrick thought, "She's a nice lady. A lot nicer than her friend."

After he retrieved the cubes and plopped them into his glass, Marge broke the silence. "I'm Marge O'Connell and this, of course, is Varrick."

"Yes, we met already, Mrs. O'Connor." Without a pause, he got down to business. "I don't want to hurry you, but we need to take care of some matters before we go. And I have a commitment at five, so..." His voice trailed off as he unlatched his leather valise and withdrew some papers. Marge looked at the other three and gripped her napkin tightly, which was already wound around her right hand. She waited for him to continue.

"Here are documents I need signed before we can proceed. They're all the standard documents. They allow me to work with your son and essentially say he will be under my professional care."

The last phrase sounded so final to Marge that she momentarily balked. Wanting to read them completely, but not wishing to offend Dr. Gayle, she nodded and bent over the papers momentarily. "Just standard procedure, Mrs. O'Connor. You may read them if you like, but I assure you they're pretty standard." There was just too much print for her to take in quickly, so she made more of a show of reading the documents than actually perusing them.

As she handed them back, Marge asked, "Is that all?"
He smiled. "That's it. He'll be in good hands." Looking at Varrick, he said, "Right, Sport?"

Not knowing how to respond, Varrick couldn't summon up another shrug. It wasn't his place to judge whether he'd be in good hands or not. He didn't know this guy from the man in the moon. He was hoping his mother could see the skeptical look etched on his face, but he knew she was too nervous to notice much of anything.

"Varrick Honey, answer the man. He asked you a question and the polite thing to do is answer." Smiling and looking at Dr. Gayle, she reassured him, "I did teach him right. He just forgets from time to time. Right, Honey?"

Not knowing which question to answer, he simply said, "Yes, Mom." It seemed to appease everyone and move the conversation on to the next phase.

"Well, Mrs. O'Connell," Cindy Bevins said brightly and expectantly, "do you have any questions for us before we go our separate ways?" The starkness of the phrase "separate ways" was not lost on Marge or her son. Varrick discovered a large lump in his throat and tried hard to swallow it away, but was unsuccessful. *I'm being led to the slaughter*, he thought, *and there's nothing I can do to stop it.*

Marjorie paused. "No, I don't think so. I assume I can call anytime I need to, and Varrick can call me anytime also?"

"Uh, sure. Anything else?"

Marge confined her questions to specific ones about the food and recreation at the facility. Gayle waved his hand and said, "It's one of the finest medical facilities in North America. Barrack will be in good hands, believe me."

All three winced at his mispronunciation, but thought better of correcting him. He was, after all, the most educated of the group and who were they to correct him?

Since Marge had already paid her check, there was nothing left for anyone to do but stand and prepare to leave. Trudging out to the parking lot, Varrick walked even slower than he had on the way in. He wasn't in any hurry to be left in the company of strangers and leave his only living parent, possibly not to see her again for months.

After an all-too-quick hug, Varrick and Marge said their goodbyes. Varrick crawled into the backseat of Paul Gayle's 1958 Studebaker and received the small suitcase that Marge handed him. There was no room in the car for it except on his lap, where it lay for the four-hour non-stop trip to Napa County.

Chapter

22

It wasn't so bad that I had to scrunch into the back of Doctor Gayle's car and stare at the back of his and Miss Bevins' head for four hours, but leaving Mom and not knowing when I'd see her again was the pits.

I'll be honest – I was terrified, but there was also a calm somewhere within me. Seeing Dad helped me more than I can explain. It was as if he had given me my confidence back, and a sense of peace settled over me like a warm, comforting blanket. Sure, I knew there were plenty of situations in my life that were scary, but now I didn't feel alone anymore. Someone was always with me – not just Dad's spirit, but also the Spirit of God.

It was super tough leaving my mom in that parking lot in Fresno, but I had absolutely no choice. She told me that working with Dr. Gayle was what I needed in order to get straightened out and headed on the right track. And since I'm just a kid and don't have any say in the matter, I have no choice but to go along with the program.

The ride to Napa went on forever, especially since there was nothing to do but stare at the flat, endless Central Valley gliding by. I didn't talk with either Dr. Gayle or Miss Bevins very much. Doctor G said we'd have "plenty of opportunity to talk" later. For some reason he wasn't in much of a mood to talk to Miss Bevins either, but he did whisper to her from time to time. I couldn't make out anything he said, but it seemed serious and personal. Miss Bevins would get really stiff whenever Doctor Gayle talked to her like that. After one stretch of his whispering, Miss Bevins held her hand up as if to tell him to stop. She then turned her head for the first time and looked at me in a sad way before smiling quickly and facing forward again. I was confused by all this because I thought psychiatrists and counselors were really good at listening to people's problems, but Dr. G and Miss Bevins were having lots of trouble doing that. Like I said before, I'm just a kid and don't really understand this stuff. All I know is it got really boring just holding my suitcase on top of my knees and wondering what was waiting for me in Napa.

◎ ◎ ◎

Marge clutched the wheel of her '62 Impala so tightly that her olive hands turned white. She stared into the parking lot glare without blinking. Her mind focused on the scene she couldn't see – the interior of a Studebaker headed for St. Helena. She worried about a million things: Varrick's comfort in the cramped backseat, how Cindy Bevins and Doctor Gayle would treat him, whether he had food and water. Mostly, she was racked with guilt for giving her only son over to a couple she didn't know well.

For a moment her grip slackened and she looked left and then right, contemplating chasing after the ugly, round car driven by the ugly, round-headed psychiatrist who came highly recommended by a woman she barely knew. She took a quick breath and held it. *After all,* she told herself, *we did sign some kind of legal document, and he is licensed. And psychiatrists are bonded, aren't they?* She wasn't sure. In fact, she was sure of only one thing: she wouldn't rest easy until her son was back home safe.

◎ ◎ ◎

Varrick sat cross-legged on his new bed and wrote in a clothbound book given him by Paul Gayle:

First Day: July 12, 1965

I just checked in. In fact, Dr. Gayle took care of most of that for me. Then, I got my room. It's really boss! I've never had my own room with a real bed before. And it has a TV that Dr. Gayle said I could watch during "free time." The room is bigger than mine at home, and I won't have Deirdre busting in on me at all hours demanding to watch TV while I try to sleep. It's clean and nice and has a desk, a dresser, and a window looking out on a courtyard.

And Doctor G – that's what he wants me to call him – has been really nice since we got here. He gave me this journal and told me to write in it everyday. I asked him what I should write and he said, "That's up to you. Write your feelings, observations, thoughts, whatever you want to write about." So, that's why I'm writing. Well, I'm getting ready for dinner and then Doctor G is going to start interviewing me. It sounds fun, like when Miss Bevins interviewed me a couple of weeks ago.

That's about it. I get to call Mom tonight after dinner. I hope everything is okay back home.

◎◎◎

Marjorie sat alone in her kitchen once again second-guessing a decision she'd made regarding her children. She had asked a lady from work with daughters the same ages as Deirdre and Tess if they could spend the night. Since she didn't know what time she'd be back from Fresno, she wanted them to be somewhere safe. But now she wished she'd had them stay at a neighbor's until she got home. She needed their company. As she wiped her eyes, the phone rang.

It was Varrick. He sounded good, like his old self. She thought, *Wow! This Doctor Gayle must be really good if Varrick's already feeling better. He not only got to the hospital safely, he's in a large, private room that sounds like a dormitory in a posh college. Who knows? Maybe this experience will be exactly what he needs.*

Chapter

23

Cindy Bevins approached the nurses' station in the children's psychiatric ward and asked for Paul Gayle.

"You mean *Doctor* Gayle," The head nurse corrected.

"Yes, Doctor Gayle. Sorry." She'd forgotten that Paul insisted everyone refer to him by his title whenever he was on duty. It usually didn't matter to her, but today it rankled her a bit. After all, she would soon be Mrs. Gayle. It seemed silly that she should also have to follow convention. Maybe she would insist after they marry that everyone, including Paul, call her 'Mrs. Doctor Gayle.' She smiled at her little joke. It was her first smile since the ride up from Fresno when she'd turned to look at Varrick.

The head nurse, whose name was Hedda, said, "Take a seat, Miss. I'll let the doctor know you are here."

"Thank you. May I use your restroom?"

"The restrooms are exclusively for patients. However, I will make an exception this time, Miss..."

"Bevins, soon to be Gayle." She held up her left hand to display her engagement ring and smiled for the second time in a minute, enjoying the moment.

While perched on the toilet, Cindy heard a voice - far away and sounding like a boy's. It sounded hopeful, happy, and engaged in some fun activity. Instead of flushing immediately, Cindy tiptoed over to the wall separating the men's and women's lounges and heard what sounded like a play-by-play commentary of a baseball game:

"Whitey Ford, from the stretch. Whitey checks the runner at first, gets his sign from Yogi Berra, checks the runner again, winds, and throws A HUMMER OF A FASTBALL THAT WILLIE DAVIS SWINGS AT AND MISSES! The Yankees win the Series! The Yankees win the Series! Whoa, Nellie! Whitey Ford no-hits the National League Champion Los Angeles Dodgers to close out the 1965 World Series! Can you believe it?"

There was then a soft white noise that was a boy's impersonation of a crowd roaring its approval. Turning on her heel to return to her stall to flush, Cindy giggled. "Varrick O'Connell. What an imaginative kid! Paul should have a blast working with him."

When Cindy returned to the nurses' station, Hedda Nurse (Paul's name for her) approached and said, "I'm sorry, but Doctor Gayle is in the middle of a lengthy session with a patient and cannot be disturbed for quite some time."

Cindy wanted to interject, "Yeah, he's really busy with a patient. The boy's in the restroom playing an imaginary baseball announcer," but she didn't want to get into it with either 'Hedda' or Paul. "Thank you. Tell Paul I will see him later."

◎ ◎ ◎

The next evening, Marge received a call she thought was from her son. Instead, it was Gladys - the gal who babysat the girls so Marge wouldn't need to worry about them when she went to Fresno. Gladys didn't have much to say that interested Marge, just gossip and neighborhood news. When she got a word in edge-wise, Marge explained that Varrick would be calling soon from the hospital and that she was waiting for his call. Gladys said she understood and that she'd talk to her later. Marge thought: *She only shut up because she wants to get more dirt on us.*

Before she had a chance to collect her thoughts, the phone rang. It was Varrick. "Hi, Son. How are you doing?"

"Great. Everything's hunky-dory here. How 'bout you and my lovely sisners? (As long as Marge could remember, Varrick had referred to the girls as his 'lovely sisners.')

"We're fine, Honey." They chatted awhile, but soon ran out of things

129

to talk about. So she thought she'd just pass on a couple of items from Gladys. "Varrick, I guess there was a fire today, just down the Boulevard. Remember BBQ's?"

Varrick swallowed hard, almost choking in the process. "I sure do. Did it burn down?"

"No, just some outbuildings in back. One caught fire and the flames spread to a couple of other buildings."

Varrick slumped onto the stool next to the phone in the nurses' station. He steadied his head by propping it up with his free hand. He felt dizzy, but didn't want anyone thinking there was anything wrong.

"Did anyone die?"

"There was evidence someone was living in the building that burned, but they don't know for sure if he died."

"*He?*"

"What's that?"

"You said 'he.' Was it a boy – er - I mean, a man?"

"They think it was just a bum, Honey."

Marge was stunned by what happened next. Varrick suddenly cut their conversation short and hung up before she could ask what was wrong. *Everything seems to be going really well up there, so he probably had to give the phone up to someone. It's probably like a dorm where there's only one phone available. He'll call tomorrow night and we can catch up some more.*

◎ ⊙ ◎

After slamming the receiver down, Varrick ran across the foyer area by the nurses' station and burst into his room. He sobbed facedown on his bed. Hedda softly went to Varrick's closed door and listened to his sobs. She called Paul Gayle at his on-site apartment and told him what she'd seen. "I'll be right over" was all he said.

◎ ⊙ ◎

"George, you've got to help me, George, you've got to help me, George, you've got to help me, George…" Varrick pleaded continuously

130

in a rhythm that reminded Paul Gayle of a train locomotive. He stood outside the boy's room and debated whether to talk with him now or not.

I've got to dive in headfirst early tomorrow. He's more delusional than I thought, he told himself as he turned without entering and returned to his bungalow.

◎ ⊙ ◎

Paul Gayle's research had previously consisted of five- and ten-year studies involving large numbers of boy subjects. He hadn't worked with them individually, but had always left the fieldwork to his assistants, including Cindy. But this situation was different. He would have to establish a rapport both professional and personal with this young boy in order to learn enough to write a case study, complete with diagnoses and prescribed therapies. This realization he found frightening *and* intriguing; intriguing because of the attraction of observing one boy's internal world first-hand, frightening because he'd always been wary of becoming close to young boys for fear that he might like them too much. And he liked Varrick O'Connell more than any boy he'd ever worked with.

◎ ⊙ ◎

At exactly 7 am Tuesday, Dr. Gayle summoned Varrick to his bungalow for their first session. In order to 'maintain a pure professional atmosphere,' he insisted Cindy stay at a local motor lodge. He promised to pay all of her expenses. He'd let her know when he and Varrick would be finished. "How long do you think it will be?" she asked.

"I'll tell you when it's over," he had abruptly replied. Cindy Bevins was put off by both the coldness of his tone and facial expression.

Varrick was ushered into Dr. Gayle's parlor by Hedda Nurse. Gayle firmly exclaimed, "Hold all of my calls unless it's a dire emergency. And then it better be someone's life at stake or it will be yours too." Hedda nodded and left them alone.

"Varrick," he started without greeting or pleasantry, "we have a great

131

deal to accomplish. You are not well and I need to find out why as soon as possible. Is that clear?"

Varrick had no idea how to respond, so he shrugged.

"I'll give you a battery of tests and discuss a variety of topics with you. I need you to be upfront at all times. The more cooperative you are, the quicker we'll solve this puzzle and you can be released to go home. Agreed?"

Fighting the urge to shrug again, he summoned the energy to say "Yes."

"Any questions?"

"Uh, no."

"Good. Have a seat on this couch or lie down if you like and we'll get started."

◎ ◉ ◎

Larry Jasper stood on the dirt shoulder of a remote section of Yucca Highway sixty miles from Los Angeles and held out his right arm as the third car in an hour approached. A '57 Chevy Bel Air carrying four teenage boys slowed without pulling onto the shoulder. Since it was already hot, the windows were down. The front passenger, a boy with a blonde pompadour haircut, stuck his head out. "Hey, where are you headed, Man?"

Larry brightened and said, "LA."

The boy replied, "Well, good luck, nigger boy."

The driver piped up, "Yeah, we don't pick up niggers. Sorry, but it's our official policy." He smiled broadly, held up his middle finger, and stomped on the gas pedal. As the Chevy roared off, four hands emerged from the windows and "saluted" Larry.

He knew better not to react, so he turned and waited for the next car. *I guess it's not a whole lot different than Louisiana*, he thought as he continued his vigil.

◎ ◉ ◎

Paul Gayle sat where he felt most comfortable when talking with clients and colleagues – behind his massive mahogany desk. He knew most experts in his field considered it poor form, but he reasoned he hadn't gotten to where he was by following "the book." Besides, he was better able to take notes on a desk than on his lap. He was also within fingertips' reach of his trusty tape recorder, which he definitely would use a great deal with Varrick O'Connell. Switching on the reel-to-reel, he began with an extensive word association exam, proceeded to give a Rorschach, then a wood block test, a pictorial IQ test, and a 250-question sentence completion exam. The tests took the entire day.

◉ ⊙ ◎

Around 5:30, Paul stretched in his leather high-backed chair, yawned, and asked, "What would you like for dinner?"

Varrick was exhausted from the ten-and-a-half hour session and was having trouble understanding why Dr. Gayle was taking his order for dinner since he'd been eating in the cafeteria three times daily and assumed that they were going to quit for the day and eat there.

"We're not through?"

Paul chuckled. "Yes, we're through – with testing. While you're eating I'll have someone score the tests and I'll evaluate them. Then, young man, I will proceed with lots of Q's and A's to become better acquainted with you. Okay? What'll it be – creamed chicken or chipped beef?"

Varrick swallowed hard and thought: *My two least favorite dishes on the face of the earth, besides liver and onions.* "Can I have something else, Doctor Gayle?"

"Uh, uh, uh. Who am I?"

"Doctor G?"

"That's me. Yes, you can have something else if you like. Let me call the kitchen. Hi. What's on the bill of fare besides the specials? Great. Cook up two full orders with extra onions, please. Thanks."

Before the words tumbled out of Gayle's mouth, Varrick knew he was doomed. "Guess what? We're having good old-fashioned grilled liver and onions."

Varrick lowered his head and sighed.

Chapter

24

For over an hour, Marge O'Connell debated calling the hospital. It was ten and Varrick hadn't called. The girls were in bed and she could only hear the ticking of the oven clock. Standing behind the chair Varrick sat in for meals, she thought of how much she missed him when the brrrrrinnngggg of the phone caused her to jump.

On the third ring, she was composed enough to answer. She was greeted with the most somber of voices: "This is Dr. Gayle. I have your son and he wants to speak with you."

If the caller hadn't identified himself, she would've thought he was a kidnapper calling from his hideout.

"Hello? Varrick? Are you there?"

When he came on the line there was an awkward silence because he had missed his mother's greeting. With Gayle standing behind him literally breathing down his back, he became wooden and tentative. "M-mom? Ar- are you there?"

"Honey? Didn't you hear me?"

"Uh, no."

"How are you? You sound funny."

Not wanting to frighten her, he forced himself to sound perky. "Oh, no. It's just a little past my bedtime."

Her concern level fell, but it was still that of a worried mother's. "Honey, don't they have a curfew? I need to talk to the doctor about putting you to bed earlier."

Varrick was at the age where advocating for himself was becoming necessary. He whispered emphatically into the receiver, "No, don't do that. It's okay, really."

"Are you eating healthy foods?"

"We had liver and onions tonight."

"Oh, good." She'd forgotten it was his least favorite dish and had been known to make him sick.

He knew from her tone she was now satisfied concerning his health. Feeling she had covered the important bases, she proceeded to lighter topics. "Are you able to play?"

"Uh, yes. We have a regular exercise and recreation schedule. We even have a pool table and ping-pong. Too bad Larry isn't here to play me."

"Whatever happened to that boy?"

"He's probably somewhere good," Varrick managed to say before choking up a little. *Probably with Dad and Jack Bryant* is what he'd wanted to add.

When Marge asked Varrick about his bowel movements – BM's she called them – the boy was ready to end their conversation. "Uh, I better go to bed now, Mom. I'll talk to you tomorrow night, hopefully a little earlier. 'Night."

"Good night, Sweetie. Say 'hello' to Dr. Gayle. Bye."

Not eager to face Gayle so quickly, Varrick stayed on the phone fifteen seconds longer and pretended, "Okay, Mom. You take care. Everything's fine. Don't worry. Bye."

◎ ⊙ ◎

Paul Gayle reviewed the test results in his office while having his morning cup of coffee. He wasn't surprised to find that Varrick had a high IQ – 141 to 145 on the written test and 140 to 144 on the wood block test. The Rorschach results were in the normal range, but the word association and sentence completion tests could be interpreted to show Varrick was overly preoccupied, maybe even obsessed by images of death, especially ghosts and the spirits of departed loved ones. His interest in films, comic books, and TV shows featuring angels and ghosts was certainly an indication of emotional instability and a belief in supernatural phenomena. There were also too many father-oriented

135

responses on some of the tests. It was clear Varrick needed an adult male influence in his life - a mentor, a guide, a comforter.

◎ ⊙ ◎

Varrick welcomed the opportunity to walk around the Napa State Hospital grounds. He was hoping to meet some of the other kids, maybe recruit and organize a baseball team. As he walked the redwood-lined paths, he practiced catching pop flies by tossing one of the baseballs he had brought ten, fifteen feet into the air and catching it with his glove. He toured the grounds for forty-five minutes without seeing a single kid looking remotely like a baseball player. Oh, there were kids, but they were all in wheelchairs and heavily sedated. If they could look up at all, they did so for just a moment before their heads bobbed so heavily that their chins bounced off their chests. Nurses in starched uniforms pushed them around and assisted their every effort. Varrick was both depressed and lifted by the experience. He felt sorrow for kids who may never see the outside of an institution. He also felt blessed to be so healthy and clear-headed. He counted the many blessings of his life and thanked God for each of them as he continued playing catch by himself.

◎ ⊙ ◎

Larry finally reached South-Central LA and was near where his aunt had moved from Louisiana. He squinted to read the street sign and realized he had one more block to 104th Street when he saw the strangest sight: folks carrying large items out of stores as if they were stealing them.

Having been dropped off at the Florence Ave. exit of the Harbor Freeway moments before, he hadn't been in the area long enough to know what was happening. So, he held out his hand to slow down the teenage boy who'd been running back and forth between an ancient pickup and an appliance store. "Hey! What's going on?"

The skinny, dark-skinned boy wearing only a white undershirt and blue shorts looked at Larry with surprise, "Are you serious, brother? This here's a major riot. Get what you can while you can. I gotta split, man." With that, he secured the tailgate of the '41 Ford quarter-ton truck. Larry saw five TV sets, three stereos, and a dozen smaller appliances. He stared in disbelief as the kid jumped in the passenger side and the truck roared off.

There were police around, but they stayed away from the looters and stuck close to their car radios. There was a helicopter a block away that appeared to be a radio or TV station's. 'KTLA' was painted on its side in large letters and it hovered above the scene.

Still not knowing why it was all happening, Larry left the scene as quickly as possible without running. He was sure his aunt would tell him what was happening. She probably wouldn't recognize him since it had been several years since they'd seen each other back home, but he figured he could convince her of his identity. He just couldn't believe the scene around him. After all, he'd heard Watts was a pretty cool place. Walking resolutely, but not too quickly past the LAPD squad car, he headed for Aunt Essie's.

◎ ◎ ◎

When Varrick returned from his stroll around the grounds, he checked in with Hedda at the front desk. " Dr. Gayle will see you now. Put your ball and glove here and I'll put them in your room. Doctor Gayle has a full day planned so you better get started."

Varrick laid his glove and ball on her counter and walked like a condemned man to his meeting with 'Doctor G.'

As Varrick entered, Paul Gayle said without looking up, "Close the door and have a seat." He spent the next fifteen minutes finishing his notes before joining Varrick on the couch. He sat so that their knees touched.

Speaking softly, Paul Gayle said, "We will now speak informally. I'll ask you a few questions, but we'll generally just talk about what is on your mind."

Gayle's questions dealt with topics Varrick felt awkward talking about: his father's death, arguments with his sister Deirdre, recent conversations he had had with George and his dad, and conflicts with the Krupt brothers. Varrick cooperated, but it was difficult for him to speak freely to someone he hardly knew. In answer to Gayle's questions, he gave the minimal amount of data. It didn't matter, though, because Gayle would build on each answer and trap him into corners where it was impossible not to give much more information. It was a long, grueling process that Varrick could not see the end of.

After three hours of nonstop 'Q and A', Varrick stretched his neck by tilting his head to each side. Paul set down his clipboard and asked, "Is your neck stiff?" When Varrick nodded, Gayle said, "Here, let me help." He had him turn away and began massaging his neck. After five minutes of silent massage, he had Varrick lay facedown on the couch and worked on his entire back. As he sensed Varrick relax, Gayle asked the same question, but in a more casual way.

Varrick lay facing the back of the coffee-colored couch and felt himself drifting off to sleep. The massage and the cool office succeeded in relaxing him for the first time in months. But it all ended a few moments later when Varrick awoke to the sensation of something hovering above. It was Doctor Gayle kissing his face. Varrick's first inclination was to bolt upright, but he knew that that probably wasn't the best way to escape the clutches of a strange man.

He lay there and tried thinking of a strategy that would get him out of this situation. All he could think of was to pretend to be asleep and then bolt upright and pretend to have awakened from the kissing and ask what was going on. And that's what he tried to do, but it didn't work completely. Paul caught him in mid-spin and pinned down both his shoulders with his hands.

"Quiet!" he whispered. "Hey, would you like to play a game?"

Varrick certainly didn't feel like playing anything with this strange man, but his options had narrowed since his attempt to escape had been thwarted. "What game?"

Gayle smiled, his facing getting redder and the veins in his forehead and around his temples beginning to bulge from the effort of keeping him pinned. "It's called 'Show and Tell.' Have you played it before? Maybe in school?"

Varrick knew he shouldn't respond, so he continued staring at Gayle's reddening face. "You show me yours and then I'll show you mine. Okay?" Staring at the doctor's face for a couple more seconds as if he were trying to decide, he inhaled as slowly and fully as he could before letting loose the loudest scream of his life. There was a great deal of violent thrashing around, mainly on Doctor Gayle's part, and before Varrick knew what was going to happen next, everything turned black.

The next images were very dark and shadowy and took a full minute for Varrick to figure out that he was lying in bed in his room. A strap had been fastened across his chest and a similar but double-looped belt held his ankles in place. He had no idea what time it was, but knew it was dark out. Seated in a wing-backed chair that had been brought in from somewhere else was a man with a familiar round head. He sipped from a short glass holding a clear drink with a slice of lime. "Did you enjoy your rest?" he asked as if nothing had happened.

"I want to talk to my mother," was all Varrick could make himself say.

Paul Gayle eventually answered, "*I* will talk with your mother. I have news for her and some matters to discuss with her as well."
He stretched both arms while still holding his drink. "Well, you better get your rest and avoid any excitement."

Seeing that he was rising to leave, Varrick spoke up. "Wait a minute. What if I have to go to the bathroom?"

"Oh," he laughed, "I took care of that. Until you start acting your age again, you'll wear diapers. So, feel free to 'go to the bathroom' anytime you like." He laughed and left, locking the door behind him.

Chapter

25

Marjorie O'Connell awoke to the ringing of her phone. She twisted to read her alarm clock, which then went off. Switching it off, she fumbled for the receiver on the end table. "Yes?"

"Mrs. O'Connell?"

"Yes. Who is this?"

"Doctor Gayle, Mrs. O'Connell."

"Is everything all right?"

"That's why I'm calling. Do you have a few minutes?"

Marge sat up and swung her feet over to her slippers and managed to slip them on without using her hands. "If it has to do with my son, I have all the time in the world."

"Good. This shouldn't take long. My staff and I have spent considerable time working with your son, testing and evaluating him at first and now interviewing him thoroughly so we can have as clear of a picture of his personality as possible." Paul paused for a moment to choose his wording carefully before launching into the crux of the matter. "We have had a couple setbacks. Varrick has had two interludes of outbursts that we have had to address. One of them was last night and that's why I'm calling to let you know."

Marge's mind swirled with questions. "Is he okay? May I speak with him?"

"That's what I wanted to talk with you about. Varrick has not been in a rational frame of mind to speak with anyone the past twenty-four hours. Right now he's sedated and resting. He has been very difficult to deal with these past two days and if things don't improve soon, we may have to take measures to get him back on an even keel."

"What exactly are you suggesting, Doctor?"

"I'm suggesting we try an intervention that will bring him back emotionally and psychologically."

Waiting for the doctor to elaborate, Marge was forced to ask, "And what would that be?"

"It's a new procedure called electro-shock therapy. It has been quite successful with patients suffering from delusions, depression, and outbursts such as Varrick has been having."

"I see. I'm not a doctor, but all of this seems premature. When can I speak with my son?"

"I assure you, this is an intervention proven safe and effective in fighting depression and delusions."

Marge was stunned into silence. What was she going to do? Buy time. That's it – she would ask for more time to think about it. "Doctor Gayle, this is something very new and unexpected for both my son and me."

"I understand, but we believe this is the best possible intervention for him under the circumstances."

"Is this something we have to decide right now? Can I have time to think? I'd also like to speak with Varrick."

Now it was time for Gayle's mind to whirl with possibilities. *There's no way I can let her speak with him. He'll tell her what went on, she'll report me, and I could lose everything. I'll stonewall her.*
"Mrs. O'Connell, may I call you Marjorie?"

There was no answer. Marge was stunned by the question and felt it was a ruse to divert her attention away from the subject of her son.

"Mrs. O'Connell," Gayle started again, "I was calling you out of courtesy. I do not need your approval on which therapy I deem necessary for treating a patient. We will be proceeding as planned. Time could be of the essence."

Marge was again stunned and at a loss for words. She sat in stony silence for so long that when she finally hung up, her joints creaked from inactivity.

◎ ◎ ◎

Cindy Bevins was watching the news in her motel room when she saw the snapshot of a face that looked familiar. She turned up the volume. "Los Angeles County Sheriff Peter Pitchess has sent the following release to all newspapers, radio stations, and television stations in California: 'A twelve-year-old Negro boy, Larry Jasper, has been missing for ten days. He is five feet, nine inches tall, one hundred and sixty pounds and was last seen wearing a white t-shirt, denim pants cuffed about three inches, and white tennis shoes. There is reason to believe the boy may have perished in a fire in Yuccaville, but officials are still investigating. Anyone with information in this matter are asked to contact the Los Angeles County Sheriff's at...'"

She racked her memory before realizing where she'd seen that face. *Varrick's friend! My god, I hope he's alive and well. I wonder if Varrick knows what's going on. Of course, I can't tell him about it now. It would upset him even more than he already is.*

Cindy wondered if she would ever see her students at Joshua School again since Paul had been hinting that their wedding day was right around the corner.

⊚ ⊙ ⊚

Marge called her boss to tell him she wouldn't be coming in. The water district director trusted her implicitly. "Take today off. Fridays are slow. If you need Monday off, too, take it. With all the extra work you do, I can't in good conscience count any time you take." She thanked him and began reading the documents she'd signed with Doctor Gayle in Fresno, looking for loopholes that would allow her to stop the therapy. Not finding any, she broke down and cried for the first time since her husband's funeral. It didn't last long, but it purged her of some of her frustration. She could almost feel her husband's presence. "Maybe I need a psychiatrist," she mused as she put the papers back in her file cabinet in Varrick's room.

She spied the stack of journals Varrick had kept for the last three years and couldn't resist reading the most recent. What impressed her most about the entries were not the many references to George the guardian angel or even the visit from her deceased husband. What she

142

found most amazing was the realistic accounting of every detail or comment that had occurred between Varrick and Deirdre and/or Marge. Every quote was verbatim of what she could remember. She read every entry three times and still couldn't find a single mistake. She concluded that her son had reported everything as it had happened.

She knew what she had to do.

$$\circledcirc \; \odot \; \circledcirc$$

Marge drove past the Fresno city limit sign on Highway 99 and thought of stopping for lunch at the Denny's where she and Varrick had met Paul Gayle and Cindy Bevins a few days ago. As she approached the rear entrance, she heard someone calling her: "Mrs. O'Connell, is that you?" She turned toward the restaurant's trash bins and saw a figure hiding behind a corner of one of them.

Smiling nervously, she asked, "How do you know me?"

"You're Varrick's mother."

"Yes. Oh, you're Varrick's friend Larry!"

"That's right, ma'am. Are you headed for Napa?"

"I am. How did you know?"

"A lucky guess. That's where I'm headed, too."

She was flabbergasted, "How are you planning on getting there?"

Lifting up his right thumb, he said, "It's gotten me this far and I hope it gets me the rest of the way."

"Why are you going to Napa? And aren't you a runaway?"

"My best friend is there and I thought he could help me straighten my life out."

Marge was touched by his answer. Her motherly instincts kicked in. "Have you eaten?"

"Not today."

Marge brightened, "Well, let's take care of that right now. You are my guest for lunch, Mr. Jasper. We have a few things to talk over."

Larry smiled broadly. "Yes, ma'am. Allow me." He opened and held the door for her as she entered.

Marge gave the restaurant the once-over and thought: For a run-of-the-mill coffee shop, this place sure has played an important role in my life.

143

Paul Gayle sat at the small conference table with nothing but a thin file setting on it. Nurse Hedda and a short, brooding man with a crew cut sat opposite him. "So, we're all set for tomorrow, Ken?"

"First thing in the morning, Boss." Ken was the technician at the hospital best known as a 'jack of all trades' by Dr. Gayle. If an electronic test or therapy were needed, Ken Knoblock could figure it out. He wasn't the brightest star in the galaxy, but he was the most reliable for Paul Gayle. He would go to the ends of the earth for Paul, and *had* on many occasions. He never questioned Gayle's decisions or orders, but always complied. Ken was eternally grateful to Paul for giving him a job when no one else would. Who else in the business would hire and then give a great amount of trust to a convicted felon and an ex-patient of Napa State? Paul Gayle had, and Ken had benefited from Paul taking that risk many times. Ken had dutifully done much of Paul Gayle's dirty work over the past decade. This was a minor chore compared to many jobs Paul had given him and he was only too glad to do it for his boss.

"Good," Dr. Gayle continued. Looking at his right-hand person, he asked, "Everything ready for tomorrow, Hedda?"

"Yes, Doctor, everything's set for six am. Do you want the boy to spend tonight in his room or the juicer?"

Paul laughed at her name for the electroshock room, but stopped when he saw no smile on her face. He knew too well how seriously she took her job. "Don't do anything out of the ordinary. In the morning, let's just wheel him in."

"Yes, Doctor."

"Thank you. See you both tomorrow bright and early." As they left, he marveled at their dedication to him. "Loyalty is always number one with me," he mused as they left him alone in the dimly lit room.

26

After checking in at the front gate, Marge parked in a remote corner of the hospital lot. She took a deep breath and then fixed her hair while using the rear-view mirror. "Larry, this won't be easy. There could be trouble from Dr. Gayle and his staff. If you want to stay here, I'll understand." She was hoping, however, he would insist on joining her. With his size, he could be good backup. Staff would never suspect this man-sized person was only a lad.

"I'll do anything to help Varrick or his mother." The look in his eye persuaded her that he would.

⊙ ⊙ ⊙

Cindy Bevins sat in the tiny waiting area of the children's ward and checked her watch. She knew it was quitting time, but still no sign of Paul. She knew she wouldn't get anywhere with Hedda Nurse, so she simply smiled when Hedda looked up from her desk, where she sat as though enthroned as a royal.

Paul Gayle's office door swung open and he escorted Marge O'Connell and a man toward the front door. "I can't let you see him now, but perhaps tomorrow at 4:00."

Cindy stood, wanting to say 'hi' to Marge, but knowing better than to interrupt Paul. Marge said just loud enough for Cindy to hear, "We've come all this way and don't understand how a short visit would harm him."

When Cindy focused on the face of the person with Marge, she gasped and approached them. "Good afternoon, Marge. Larry? Larry Jasper? Is that you?"

Larry looked down and said softly, "Yes, ma'am."

"I thought so. I'm sure Varrick will be glad to see you." Paul Gayle shot her a stern look that stopped her cold. An awkward silence ensued until Paul resumed his attempt at trying to usher Marge and Larry out. For the first time, Marge stood her ground with Gayle. She wasn't loud, just emphatic. "Look," her eyes flashed at his, "we're not going anywhere until I see my son."

Cindy, torn in her allegiance, knew she had information Paul would want, so she broke the cardinal law he'd laid down when she began working with him – she interrupted. "Doctor Gayle? May I see you a moment?" Without turning, he shook his head.

Marge continued. "Doctor, I will do whatever it takes to see my son. If I have to call the police, then so be it. But I will see him *today*."
Cindy knew she had to persist. "Doctor, I *really* think you need to know some information I have for you."

With a slowness that spoke volumes about Paul Gayle's arrogance and impatience with anyone who would try to interfere with any plan he might have, he turned partly toward Cindy and gave her a look that said 'This better be good.'

"May we talk in your office?"

He shrugged as if to say, 'Do I have a choice? You won't back down.'

Gayle returned to his office and left the door open for Cindy to follow. She entered and shut it firmly. "Paul, I know how you hate to be interrupted, but I thought you'd want to know this. Larry is a student at my school."

"So what? That's why you interrupted us and kept that woman another moment in my hospital?"

"He's a runaway. I saw his picture on the news. Marge O'Connell obviously drove him up here, so you might want to use that little tidbit if things get tight."

Paul Gayle smiled and his mood changed completely, "I love you, Cin. You're a lifesaver."

146

◉ ⊙ ◎

While all the commotion in the lobby was happening, Hedda thought she should check on Varrick and make sure he was still unconscious and in his restraints. Unlocking his door and slipping in, she had to wait for her eyes to adjust to the lack of light. She crept to his bedside and placed the back of her hand on his neck. His pulse was appropriate for being sedated (35) and he hadn't moved since she'd checked three hours ago. "We'll just let sleeping dogs lie." She turned and returned to her station.

◉ ⊙ ◎

"Okay," Paul Gayle began, "I'll let you see him for exactly one minute. He has been sedated, so he'll be unconscious or at least incoherent. If you're willing to abide by my conditions, I'll let you see him."

"Thanks. I have to go out to my car to bring his gift and then I'll be back." Marge smiled as if nothing negative was happening and went to her Impala with Larry.

When they got there, she looked back to make sure no one had followed. "We need a plan and I need your help."

"Larry is willing to help Varrick out of *any* jam."

◉ ⊙ ◎

After kissing Gayle on the cheek, Cindy Bevins said, "You don't mind if I join you and Marge while she sees Varrick, do you?"

Paul was ready to dismiss her when he thought that her presence might somehow smooth things over. *In fact, she may be a distracting influence if Varrick were to become conscious. He might be less likely to blurt out or act up.* "Sure, sweetie, a good idea. It won't take long, then we can go to dinner."

◉ ⊙ ◎

147

Marge got the Yankee pennant out of her trunk and turned to Larry. "We'll try Plan A and if that doesn't work, we'll go with B. Are you scared?"

"Mrs. O'Connell, I've had some situations lately that were way more scary than some man in a white coat."

His quiet cockiness gave her the confidence she needed. They approached Dr. Gayle as if he were a friend.
He said, "I hope you don't mind if Miss Bevins joins us."

Marge beamed. "We don't mind at all." They entered and waited by the door until their eyes could adjust. Marge asked, "You don't mind if we have a little light, do you? I'm afraid I might trip over something."

Marge adjusted the blinds so enough light entered for them to move about easier. They gathered around Varrick, who was so motionless that Marge wasn't sure he was breathing. "Doctor, do you mind if we hold his hands?"

Wanting to be rid of them, he said, "Okay, but just for a moment and then we will all have to leave."

"Okay. Larry, would you mind praying for Varrick?"
Not expecting this, but not wanting to disappoint Mrs. O'Connell, Larry grasped Varrick's left hand with both of his hands and squeezed. "Father God, we humbly thank Thee for all Thy help and guidance. We lift up our brother Varrick O'Connell and beseech Thee to heal him and bless him. Lord, we pray that Thou wilt deliver him of whatever ails him and we thank Thee in Jesus' precious name. Amen."

When Larry finished, Marge whispered, "Look!" She pointed to the spot where Cindy Bevins and Paul Gayle had stood just a moment before. "Thank You, Lord. That's just the break we need. We have got to work fast."

◎ ◎ ◎

Paul and Cindy stood by the front door and waited for Marge and Larry to finish their visit. Just when Paul was about to check on them, they emerged from Varrick's room and closed the door. Paul, hungry and anxious to go to dinner, didn't check on his patient. "Are you two staying somewhere local?"

"It looks like we may have to," Marge said simply.

With that, the four headed out to the parking lot. Marge waited until Paul Gayle's MG exited the lot before she followed it.

Paul speed shifted and was well ahead of Marge when he got to Highway 29 and turned toward town. Marge was able to track him and follow a half-mile behind. She spotted his sports car in front of a French restaurant and parked a block away. "As soon as it's dark enough, we'll head back."

◎ ⊙ ◎

Paul Gayle had purposely not told anyone where he and Cindy would be dining. He didn't want staff interrupting him while he told his fiancé of his plan for them to elope the next week. He was going to take his time and, after they'd enjoyed a bottle of Napa Valley's finest Cabernet, he'd spring his wedding-in-Reno plans on her.

◎ ⊙ ◎

Varrick was again dreaming about the Krupt boys. They had made their way to Napa, were trying to kidnap him and take him back to Yuccaville. It truly was a nightmare because Varrick couldn't decide what fate was worse – staying tied up in a bed and being seen daily by Doctor G or being kidnapped by the evil band of Krupt Brothers.

In the dream, they were breaking in through the window. He was about to scream when he noticed that both of the brothers holding him were actually being gentle. And one of them even sounded like his mother, so he didn't fight at all. It wasn't until he'd been deposited in the back seat of a car like his mother's Chevy Impala that he realized this was no dream; this was an answer to prayer.

Chapter

27

It was bizarre being on the road all night and feeling "loopy" from the sedatives, but there was nowhere on earth I'd rather be than in the backseat of our Chevy Impala riding home with my mother and best friend. For the first time since Dad was alive, my mom was actually relaxed. She was very nice to Larry, who was his usual kind, gentlemanly self. Mom thanked him several times for supporting her at Napa State, and though he kept saying it had been no "big deal," I could tell her gratitude meant a lot to him. No one had ever made a fuss over him before, so this was all new and he 'took to it like a dog to a bone,' as he liked to say.

I didn't want to ruin the ride home, so I waited for a couple days to tell Mom about what Dr. Gayle tried to do to me in his office. The same officers who had questioned me before were the ones who came to take the report. Doctor G was arrested on charges of attempted child abuse, child endangerment, and unlawful imprisonment. Miss Bevins was interviewed by the Sheriff's office and reported that Dr. Gayle had kept me in the hospital against my will.

When we arrived in Yuccaville, the sun was just starting to peek over the buttes. Mom and Larry helped me out of the car, up our steps, and into my room, but I didn't need their help as much as I let them think. Mom let Larry sleep in my room with me. Since my pullout couch is queen-sized, there was plenty of room for both of us.

Before Larry and I awoke, Mom had already made some calls and had amazing news. "I called Social Services and told them about my picking up Larry hitch-hiking and his staying here last night. They're aware of his case and told me that they have new information that resulted in the

Hickses having their foster license suspended and even possibly revoked and the other boys being removed from the home. They've been placed in a group home together and Larry is invited to join them. It's here in Yuccaville, so they won't have to leave Joshua School."

Larry looked equally relieved about not having to be on the lam and the boys being in a safe place, but I could tell he was still unsettled. I didn't want to put him on the spot and ask him, especially in front of my mom, but he jumped right in and told us: "Larry and his brothers need somewhere permanent, somewhere they can call home until they grow big and are on their own. The system can eat kids up, especially the little ones."

My mom smiled. "I made some calls this morning regarding you and your brothers and guess what? I found a couple who recently lost their only child and they've expressed interest in starting a foster home and perhaps adopting in the future. I know it would have to be okay with you and your brothers and Social Services, but I know these people and can't think of anyone who would do a better job of caring for kids. Varrick, tell Larry about the Bryants."

I felt a sensation inside me so warm that I knew it was from God. He was answering several prayers in one fell swoop. As much as I would have loved for Larry to live with us, I knew it wouldn't be practical. Plus, the other boys needed their 'big Bubba' who'd been the only family they'd ever really known. I thought of each boy, but I focused on little Rosy. Being the youngest and having the added burden of being 'twice different' as Larry described him, Rosy needed Larry the most. Larry couldn't protect him from all the evils of the world, but he could ward off a lot of them, just like he had for me.

I've been back from Napa a month and things have settled down. First, we had our special 'Jack Bryant Memorial Game' for charity against the Leviathans three days after my 'big escape.' It was played at our regular field, but they brought in bleachers from the Pony League field for the extra people who showed up. According to the announcer on KUPI, there were 650 in attendance, pretty good for a small town.

Two really neat things happened before the game started. First, we had a moment of silence for Jack, and I was asked to say a prayer. It was really tough and I told my mom I didn't know how I was going to do it, but I made it through somehow. There hadn't been any more visits from George or Dad or Jack to give me strength, but I felt the presence of the Almighty before, during, and after the prayer. They had a microphone set up at home plate. The Eagles lined up along first base since we were considered the home team and the L's stood on the third base line. Coach Rodriguez was at my right side giving me support, as I was getting ready to start. The person on my left I'll talk about in a little bit.

I walked up to the microphone stand and everyone suddenly got quiet. Then, the league president said over the PA, "Let's observe a moment of silence for Jack Bryant, who lost his life to Leukemia last month. His courage and strength will always be remembered."

The silence seemed to go forever even though I'm sure it wasn't more than a minute. In the middle of the collective silence, when we could have heard even a pin drop on the dirt field, a voice rang out, "We'll miss you, Jackie." I thought I was going to lose it right then. A lump the size of a Washington apple formed in my throat and I started to panic about having to speak in the next few seconds. Coach Rodriguez patted me on the back and then gave me a hug. "Eet's okay, amigo," he whispered. All I could do in response to his support was simply nod.

The League President spoke again. "And now a prayer from Jack Bryant's friend and teammate, Varrick O'Connell." I took a deep breath, bowed my head, closed my eyes, took another deep breath, and said: "Father God, thank You for today, and thank You for every day that Jack Bryant lived on this earth... Even though he was only ten, he lived a full life... He gave everything his best effort, never complained, and was always there when I needed something. He was the best friend I ever had and I know he was the best son his parents could've had. This game is in your memory, Jackie... I know you're watching. I love you, little buddy, and I'll miss you more than words can say. Thank You, Lord, for the gift You gave us of a life that shined so brightly that it lives today and will continue burning as long as there is love in the world. Amen."

The lump in my throat returned and I got the worst case of the "crybabies," but what can you expect? Coach R gave me another hug and then the person on my left said, "Larry loves you, Man. Wish I could have as good a friend as Jack had."

He bear hugged me and I looked at him and said, "You do, Brother." He laughed and said, "I know I do, you dodo head." I looked at him in shocked wonder. He continued, "Aren't you supposed to say 'that's Mr. Dodo head to you'?"

I had trouble forming my words I was so stupefied. "How did you know about Mr. Dodo head?"

He smiled and said, "You're not the only one around here who knows folks in high places." He walked back to the dugout before I could say anything.

Oh, yeah. I need to tell you why Larry was there. The Bryants applied for a temporary foster home license and have been taking care of Larry and his 'brothers.' The Bryants' only request for the game was that Larry be allowed to play in Jack's place. Although Larry Jasper and Jack Bryant had never met, there was a connection between the two of them that no one has ever been able to figure out.

And now on to the game. I'd love to say Larry was the hero and won it for us, but that wouldn't be the truth. He did help us a lot - not on the field, but in the dugout cheering us on and keeping things light. After all, Jack's death had brought down the entire team, especially because he had been our biggest cheerleader. Larry has the same basic personality, so it was only natural that he joined us for this game to cheer us on.

As you might have guessed, Ross Ramsey pitched for the Leviathans. He was his usual overpowering self and still had us mastered. He wasn't no-hitting us like before, thanks to a perfectly executed drag bunt, but he was shutting us down fairly well. After three innings, the L's held a one-nothing lead thanks to Big R hitting another homer over my head in center.

At the end of the third, Coach R gathered us together and said, "Hey boys, you keen beat these guys. I know you can. I keen feel it in my bones. And my bones don't lie." Even though he was as serious as a heart attack, we all busted up - everyone but Larry Jasper.

Larry shook his head and said, "Listen, guys. Coach is right. You *can* beat these guys. And you know what? You *will* beat them. You know why? Because you owe it to Jack Bryant and you owe it to his parents who are out there in the stands and you owe it to your coach here who's been with you through thick and thin.

But, most of all, you owe it to yourselves. So, don't be laughin' about Coach's bones." He looked at Coach, grasped his left arm, pulled his elbow up to his ear, and said, "I can hear it! I can hear victory in the man's bones. And so can you if you'll just believe."

With that, we each filed by Coach Rodriguez, held up his elbow and listened for victory. We marched resolutely out to the field for the beginning of the fourth and chattered so loudly and enthusiastically that all three batters, including Big R, struck out.

I ran to the dugout, picked out some lumber, and stepped into the on-deck circle. As I swung my bat, I heard the chain link fence rattle behind me. I turned and saw both Mr. and Mrs. Bryant smiling. Mrs. B said, "We've got something we thought might help you." She pulled a baseball bat from behind her back. "I know Jack would want you to have this, Varrick." She tried to push it through one of the openings, but it wouldn't go through, so I ran around to the end of the dugout to get it from her. "Good luck," she whispered as she gave me a big hug.

As I headed for home plate and my name was announced, I thought I heard Mr. Bryant yell, "Hit one for Jackie, Dodo head." I wanted to stop in my tracks, turn, and ask, "What did you say?" but I thought better of it. *Besides,* I thought, *I'm probably just imagining that he said that.*

I stood ten feet to the side of the batter's box watching Big R throw his last three warm-up pitches. I marveled at his speed, poise, and control. But I also marveled that I wasn't having butterflies in the pit of my stomach either. I looked at Jackie's bat, kissed it, and waved at the Bryants, still standing behind the fence next to our dugout. They waved back as the umpire yelled "Play Ball!"

I dug in, really dug in, right on top of the plate, which I know royally ticked Big R off. He gave me the meanest, dirtiest look as I finished wagging my bat and settled in. He didn't so much as glance at his catcher first for a signal, but immediately leaned back with all his might, wound up, and threw a heater right at my head!

All I remember is lying on top of home plate and coughing at the dirt that enveloped me. Some of it even got in my eyes and I called time-out to regain my sight. Coach R emerged from the dugout because in all the excitement he'd forgotten to take his usual post at the third-base coach's box. He ran up to me and asked, "You all right, Varrick? Can you continue?"

The umpire came around and looked me over, too. It was the same ump who had asked me two weeks earlier if I had been tagged by Big R. "You okay, Podner?"

I nodded, wiped dirt off my lips, gabbed my bat and gripped it determinedly, and climbed into the batter's box. Coach R pointed in Ross Ramsey's direction and said something to the ump before running out to the third-base coach's box. A small group of our players' fathers started laughing when they realized Mr. Rodriguez hadn't been minding his post. "What a stupid beaner" could be heard a couple of times above the general crowd noise.

The umpire called time out, brushed off the plate with a few whisks of his broom, pointed at Big R, and said, "I'm warning you: Do that again and I'll toss you."

Ross Ramsey remained on the mound, leered at me, and shrugged. "It was an accident," he half-yelled.

I'd like to say I hit the ball so hard at Big R that it knocked him out and he had to be taken to the hospital, but I didn't. I did take a full swing and hit the pitch, but it only dribbled back to him and he threw me out before I left the box.

Both teams went down in order in the fifth and top of the sixth.

With the scoreboard showing "Home: 0 runs, one hit, and no errors" and "Visitors: 1 run, 1 hit, and no errors," we began our last at-bat. Since I was fourth in line to bat, I had little hope of getting another chance. Fortunately (or unfortunately at the time for Bunny Youngman), the second pitch slightly nicked his bat. (Or, I should say Jack's bat, because all of us had been using it since Jack's parents had presented it to me back in the fourth inning.) Bunny looked exactly like he had every other time he'd faced Big R the past two seasons, frightened as a – well, as a little bunny. He stepped out of the box and looked at Coach for his sign. Naturally, we all thought it would be the 'hit away' sign with two strikes, but Coach gave the bunt sign and Bunny, with the aid of Jack's special bat, bunted impeccably down third and made it to first unscathed.

The next batter - our ten-year-old second-string right fielder who only

155

played because his parents demanded he get to bat at least once in the game - was up next. Big R must have been unnerved by Bunny's bunt because he walked the little guy in four pitches. Four pitches! Ramsey hadn't done that in his entire Little League pitching career.

The next batter was Larry Jasper, our honorary Eagle and left fielder. Although Larry was the most muscular kid on the field, he was also the worst batter. He had never played baseball and hadn't the instincts of a hitter. But one thing was for sure: Big R was not going to throw at his head. He pitched him very carefully and went to full count.

"Okay, Larry, you can hit this guy. Let 'er rip!" I yelled from the on-deck circle.

Larry - bless his big ol' heart - gave it his best swing, but he dribbled the ball back to the mound just as I had and, before we knew it, the runners ahead of him were out at second and third. A double play had cost us two outs and now the outcome of the ballgame was in my shaky hands.

I knelt on one leg in the circle, took in a huge breath of desert air, and prayed: "Lord, I won't ask anything for myself, but I do ask for a miracle for Jack." I strode to the plate, picked up Jack's bat, and kissed it as all of my teammates before me had.

Larry yelled from first, "Varrick, the time is now. I can hear it in the old man's bones." All I can remember hearing after that was the thumping of my heart.

"Lord," I said to myself as I stepped out and pretended to check a sign from Coach, "I know You created everything: my heart and Jack and this moment, so I'll just ask You to help me win this one for Jackie Boy." I stepped back into the batter's box, dug in as I had before, and glared at Big R. He pretended like he didn't see me or hadn't noticed my digging in, but just took his catcher's signal and wound up and let the ball fly right toward the plate.

Right then I did the weirdest thing in my life up to that point - I shut both eyes and swung as hard as my spindly arms would allow. I offered that swing up to God and left it for Him to direct, and guess what?

I made contact; good, solid contact right off the end of the bat. Since I had swung late at R's heat, the ball flew toward the left field line. The left fielder took off after it, running back and to his right until he did the most amazing thing – he put on the brakes and threw his mitt up in the air to stop it. Naturally, that didn't do the trick. It flew over his glove and continued all the way to the base of the fence. All I remember from then on is flying around the bases and Coach R waving me around third. I pushed and strained with all my will to run as fast as I possibly could. Halfway home, I saw Big R planted in front of home plate waiting for a throw from left field, probably the center fielder backing up the gloveless left fielder.

Ross Ramsey caught the ball and squared himself to tag me as I left my feet and began my hook slide. I kicked up a tremendous dust cloud and the umpire leaned in to catch the play, which he probably didn't see at all. With me lying there flat on my back on top of home plate, I looked up at the ump and asked, "Well?"

He looked me straight in the eye and asked, "Did he tag you?"

Big Ross Ramsey glared at me, bugged his eyes out, and mouthed threats at me and I said, "It doesn't matter, sir. He dropped it. Look!"

Sure enough, seven feet behind home all by itself was the ball. The umpire contorted his face even more than Ross Ramsey's and yelled, "He's safe!"

I looked down at my left knee and saw a blotch of bright red spreading over the entire area. The first Eagle to arrive was Larry, who picked me up and carried me like a baby out toward Coach R, who met us half way and said, "Your mother is definitely going to keel us this time, Panchito." He ran with Larry still carrying me and asked, "What are you going to tell her, Varrick?"

I looked at Coach, then Larry, and finally at Big R. I couldn't resist repeating Ross Ramsey's infamous words directly to him, "It was just an accident."

And *that*, dear friends, is how our humble team of Eagles beat the undefeated Leviathans. How our little team of Davids conquered (at least for one game in the summer of '65) the supposedly unbeatable team of Goliaths. And how - with the help of Dad, Jack, George the angel, and Almighty God - I beat fear for the first of many, many times to come.

Future Books by Patrick Rowlee

The following selections are upcoming releases by Patrick Rowlee. If you enjoyed reading **Varrick's Disturances**, you will likely enjoy these novels. They all feature intriguing and unique plotlines. They are at various stages of development as of Spring 2006:

Two Faces to No One – The story of two young politicians and running mates for an upcoming City Council election who are the targets of a plan to take them out of the race two weeks before voters go to the polls. At stake is not only the composition of the City Council, but the leadership of an area about to explode in size and importance.

Politicians at the national level, including the President of the United States, and figures of high standing, including the head of the most influential labor union in the country, are affected by the political rivalries and machinations that ensue.

Due to be published: Late 2006 or early 2007.

Blackballed - Craig Smart, a sportswriter for a prominent Boston newspaper, plans on interviewing the oldest living former Negro Baseball League player in the year 2010, Roscoe Braun, for an article on black baseball. Craig gets much more than he bargains for when the short human interest article becomes an extensive study into the lives of men who changed not only the face of baseball, but of classical and contemporary music, race relations, and even religion. Roscoe shares a long-kept secret with Craig that could alter the entire history of black baseball, music, and even much more.

Due to be published: 2007.

He Plays Just Like Ty Cobb – An ordinary man, who never played baseball at a level higher than Pony League, visits the National Baseball Hall of Fame in Cooperstown, New York, and begins an extraordinary journey that might result in a career in major league baseball at age forty-eight!

Possible publication: 2008.

Varrick's Disturbances Order Form

(Use this form to order Varrick's Disturbances.)

Please Print:

Name _____

Address _____

City_____ State_____

Zip_____Phone:( )_____

Email: _____

_____Copies@$12.00each$_____

Postage & handling @ $2.00 per book $_____

               Total amount enclosed $_____

Make checks payable to: Patrick Rowlee

Send to:
Patrick Rowlee
3348 Swallows Nest Lane
Sacramento, CA 95833.

For assistance: Email us at Plrowlee@cs.com

Made in the USA
San Bernardino, CA
16 June 2018